LORD SIDLEY'S LAST SEASON

Other books by Sherry Lynn Ferguson:

Quiet Meg
The Honorable Marksley

LORD SIDLEY'S LAST SEASON

•

Sherry Lynn Ferguson

AVALON BOOKS
NEW YORK

Published by Thomas Bouregy & Co., Inc.
160 Madison Avenue, New York, NY 10016

Library of Congress Cataloging-in-Publication Data

Ferguson, Sherry Lynn.
  Lord Sidley's last season / Sherry Lynn Ferguson.
      p. cm.
  ISBN 978-0-8034-9977-5 (hardcover : acid-free paper)
  1. Aristocracy (Social class)—England—Fiction.   I. Title.
  PS3606.E727L67 2009
  813'.6—dc22

                                                2009012579

PRINTED IN THE UNITED STATES OF AMERICA
ON ACID-FREE PAPER
BY HADDON CRAFTSMEN, BLOOMSBURG, PENNSYLVANIA

In loving memory of Sebastian

Chapter One

"There are few gentlemen," Colonel Bassett announced, "as useless as Sidley."

And because he spoke with such vehemence, and because he had obviously encountered too many useless gentlemen, Marian believed him utterly.

Her turn at cards was fast approaching. She had contemplated playing her nine of diamonds, but the colonel's comment caused her to forget her strategy. The whist at hand had become a puzzling mystery.

"I knew his mother, Colonel," Lady Moffett offered casually. "An adorable creature—as pretty as they come. A bit flighty, perhaps, but not unintelligent."

"Not unintelligent!" the colonel snorted. "The woman may have been brilliant, Lady Moffett, but her son's attic's to let!"

1

Lady Moffett pursed her lips. "Alicia Marsh's marriage to the earl in eighty-two was all the talk," she said. "A most unexceptionable match. There was considerable fondness as well, for 'tis rumored the earl went quite mad with grief at her death." Lady Moffett calmly plucked a card from her hand. "Do try to concentrate, Miss Marian."

"I've not met Lord Sidley." Sir Howard Napps, the colonel's card partner, spared a brief, sympathetic smile for Marian. "But he's reputed to have served with distinction at Salamanca—and then Vitoria last summer. Hardly 'useless,' Colonel. Was he not cited in Wellington's dispatches?"

"Hmm. Have you nothing else in hand, Howie?"

And as Sir Howard hastened to apologize, Marian dared ask, "Is Lord Sidley here tonight?"

"Good heavens, miss, you *have* been woolgathering!" Lady Moffett's eyebrows rose. "Have you not heard a word we've said? To think Helen Hempthorne would risk his antics! One leaves altogether too much to chance inviting Sidley. No, he's more like to be at his clubs, or the theater—or worse! Do remember my lead now," she warned.

"Sidley's parked himself over at the family place on Grosvernor Square," Colonel Bassett said, "with an army of tailors and boot makers and not a single tradesman to fix the dry rot and plaster. Fine sense of priorities that one has! With Sidley House falling to ruin about his ears! And the old country place in Kent has fared no better." He slapped a card down and took the trick, which did little to appease him. "Sidley's no longer a pup, either. Must be nearing thirty. A gentleman's obliged to show some responsibility, even if he hasn't the wherewithal. Purse-pinched, they say."

"You must own, Colonel, that he's had little time since returning home," Sir Howard noted. "Two months at most. Stands to reason he might need a new wardrobe, even to present himself to tradesmen. And then there is—well, the other matter. His circumstances . . ."

" 'Circumstances'—bah! Life is about *changing* one's circumstances! Hearts now, Howard, is it? Well! And a new wardrobe? Word is, Sidley's attempting to rival Brummell! I hear he's had ten coats from Weston—each one of 'em *black*! Useless, useless! Ah, Miss Ware, I fear you'll be regretting that very much." And with considerable relish, Colonel Bassett took the game.

Marian wished to hear more, but the card party broke up soon after. She was hurried along to make proper compliments and adieus and to depart with her older cousin, Lady Formsby, whom she affectionately called Aunt Edith, and Edith's children, Edgar and Lady Katherine.

"Katie," Marian whispered as they squeezed close in the carriage. They were almost of an age and now shared a lap rug, as the May night had turned distinctly chilly. "Who is Lord Sidley? And why would Colonel Bassett view him with such disfavor?"

"Oh, *Sidley!* Why, he's simply the most—" She caught her mother's gaze and lowered her voice to a whisper.

"'Tis all the talk, Marian. He's been in town only this spring after being out of the country altogether for—oh, many, many years. On the Peninsula. And his father took his own life, though Mama says it might have been an accident, since the late earl was so undone after his wife's passing that he could hardly have known what he was about. She's reputed to have been mad, Marian, though very beautiful. And then Sidley's elder brother, who was the heir, was killed last fall, somewhere in the Pyrenees, I think. He'd held title mere months. The Sidleys have always been wealthy, only maybe now not as much as before, and some say that Sidley himself might not be quite to rights in his mind, but it scarce signifies, because everyone *knows* he's simply top of the trees! Did I not point him out to you at the Osbornes' rout? I fear we shan't see him at any of *our* events because he is too—too elegant by half and has no inclination—that is, he simply does not appear to *care* overmuch for society. Still, he would be vastly eligible, if he were not . . . Well, something is wrong with him. No one is *quite* certain what that might be, apart from the limp, of course, which is not really so very bad, though one can't help remarking it. And Mama says we must never anticipate him at dancing, but I would so love to invite him to my ball. Perhaps Edgar might . . . Edgar!" Young Lord Formsby, seated across from them, yawned as he granted his sister his indifferent attention. "Might you manage to get Lord Sidley to my ball?"

"Sidley? To *your* ball? Not likely."

Lady Katherine frowned.

"Edgar," Marian asked, "why would Colonel Bassett have called Lord Sidley 'useless'?"

" 'Useless'? I should hardly say that he is—no more than any other gentleman, I 'spose. It's not quite the thing to be *useful* anyway, is it? Not for anyone of importance. Bassett might still be fumin' about the row over his son's curricle team. Spankin' chestnut pair. Full seventeen hands high! Sweet goers too. Went for nine hundred pounds at Tatt's a year ago. Corky Bassett lost 'em to Sidley last Thursday."

"Lost them?"

"At hazard, Cousin."

"Edgar . . ." Edith cautioned.

"What? D'you think Marian don't know a thing about gaming, Mama?" Edgar quizzed. "For all she's fresh from the country, she's no green girl."

"Indeed, I am not surprised, Aunt. I did ask. I knew there must be something. . . ."

"I fear Sidley has been gaining a most dissolute reputation, Marian. Though we are inclined to grant him much, given his—given his affliction and his disappointments. A sad history, indeed. But I have the warmest affection and regard for Sidley's aunt, Lady Adeline. And I should prefer, Katie, that you not prattle on so about Sidley, though 'tis true that more than outlandish wagers set him apart. How a gentleman chooses to spend his . . . his days is, of course, entirely his concern, but he needn't provoke the rest of us." Whereupon Edith most intriguingly firmed her lips.

Marian and Katie shared a frustrated glance. And naturally enough, how Lord Sidley chose to spend his days became a topic of some interest for several of theirs.

But when the notorious gentleman failed to gratify their curiosity by appearing at the Woodheads' musicale, or even Mr. Dudley Mandaring's much touted balloon ascension, they were compelled to consider other diversions.

Lord Sidley, however, was not to be so easily dismissed. The very next Tuesday, in pursuit of several trifling though necessary articles, Marian and her relations ventured out shopping. A desultory drizzle had kept them from taking the air that morning, and though the rain had ceased, a consequent dullness had overtaken their small company. On reaching the haberdasher's, Edgar lent Marian an obligatory hand in stepping from the carriage. But that hand was not firm enough, or perhaps not attentive enough, to counter the rain-slicked step. As her boot slipped, Marian also slipped—only to be caught and planted upright by a swift, strong arm.

"Do keep your baggage from tumbling into the street, Formsby," a low voice drawled above her. A sharply assessing blue gaze held her startled attention. But that gaze broke abruptly as her rescuer released her and turned instead to plucking with concern at a loose thread upon his otherwise immaculate coat.

"But—" Edgar protested, "but she isn't . . ."

"Baggage? Or yours?"

"Why, she certainly isn't baggage!"

"But she is yours?"

"M-m'lord! You speak of a gentlewoman! Miss Ware isn't *mine*!"

"Isn't she?" Again the blue gaze met her own. "Nevertheless, I shall be billing you for my repairs, as you appear to claim . . . propinquity." And after the shallowest of bows, her rescuer walked off in the company of two equally elegant, amused fellows.

Marian noticed that he sported a necessarily long cane, which, though he limped slightly, he utilized not at all.

"Do not mind him, Marian," Edith assured her, joining her at the curb. "He is most likely foxed. And for all he looks the gentleman, his manners are wanting. I am most disappointed."

"I shall not mind him at all—whoever he may be."

"That was Sidley," Katie claimed, her absorbed attention on the departing trio.

"He knew my name," Edgar breathed.

"Why, of course he did," Lady Formsby advised him sharply. "I suggest you both recall yourselves. Gaping in the street like ninnyhammers!"

Marian turned away with no small amount of impatience. She was above examining why she should be disconcerted. She had thought of little apart from Lord Sidley since the weekend's party. Yet now she had met him, Lord Sidley might go to the devil.

"I do envy you, Marian," Katie told her, taking her arm and squeezing it. "That Lord Sidley should rescue you! It shall be quite the *on dit*!"

"Only if you make it so, Katie. Which I would rather you did not. 'Twas nothing at all. Though I am grateful not to have fallen."

" 'Nothing'! Oh, my dear Marian, how little you know of town!"

Marian did not aspire to know much more of town. What she had seen of town had convinced her that there was too much to learn to make the effort worthwhile. She had come here to study, after all, not to debate the relative merits of Lord Sidley. And she had only six weeks at most. Her generous cousin Edith had given her this opportunity as a gift, to glean what she might from the Royal Academy's art masters and to provide some slight companionship to Katie. The girls had been a year at boarding school together, and despite nearly two years' difference in their ages, Marian felt close to her young relative. Lady Formsby had no doubt intended that Marian's steadier nature would help temper Katie's high spirits. At the very least, Katie would be encouraged to accompany Marian to a few cultural events, and that, Edith had told them mildly, must be deemed beneficial to all.

Ten days gone! Marian had so much she wished to learn and to see. Each day had become precious.

The greater part of the season had already passed, but Marian, being only too obviously the more modestly sit-

uated relation, had been rushed to the dressmakers and
milliners, so that she might partner Katie in acceptable
style. She had attended several evening events, including Helen Hempthorne's card party, and sampled ices at
Gunter's and toured the Tower. She knew how to locate
the different drawing rooms at Lady Formsby's town
house but was quite lost when attempting to navigate
much else. She felt ungrateful for spending even a moment missing her home in Northamptonshire and her
brother, Michael, newly designated curate in their village
at Brinford.

On Thursday, after spending the morning with the
drawing professor and a subsequent four intense hours
painting, Marian made a point of stopping in Piccadilly
to enter Hatchards before the shop closed. She was most
anxious for something to read. Though the Formsbys'
beautiful library boasted every other convenience, it was
surprisingly lean of books, other than Great-grandfather
Satterthwaite's sermons and every agricultural treatise
of the past century. And Katie's taste ran to startlingly
lurid literature.

At the bookstore she asked the maid to guard her paint
box and keep watch at the window for Lady Katherine
and the carriage. Then Marian eagerly sought the histo-
ries and biographies of her favorites. But she was drawn
instead to the magnificent pages in a displayed volume,
the aquatinted illustrations a miniature gallery of London's sights, and found herself happily and obliviously
employed in studying the book's riches.

"Young lady." A most superior voice invaded her perusal. Marian turned to an offended store clerk. "This is not for circulation, but a most precious volume—to be treated with utmost care." He reached to slide the book away from her reverent hands. "It is intended only for serious consideration."

"But I am considering it seriously, sir," Marian objected, making every effort to conceal her outrage. "I have been most respectful. I understood the volumes were for sale, and thus open to review."

The clerk's nose rose farther. "You intend a purchase, then?"

"Why, no. But I—"

"*I* am intending to purchase." A long, polished cane snaked across the table, staying the clerk's hands, effectively preventing the volume's removal.

Marian glanced over at Lord Sidley. Given the abruptness with which he had intervened, his manner was surprisingly easy and relaxed.

"I am an *aficionado* of such works, Mr. . . . ?"

"I am . . . I am Pinxton, my lord." The man's supercilious expression had entirely fled.

"Pinxton," Sidley repeated, starting to smile. "The young lady's opinion of this item is critical to my decision. With your permission, good Mr. Pinxton, I should like her to have sufficient time to examine the volume. 'Twould be invaluable to me that she ascertain whether 'tis truly worthwhile. And she must review anything else about that strikes her fancy. You understand? Anything that she approves, you must send 'round to me. Tonight."

"Cer-certainly, my lord."

"But only with her endorsement."

"Yes, my lord."

"And if anything should so impress her as to qualify for purchase, you will be so good as to deliver it to me yourself, then, Pinxton?"

"My pleasure, indeed, my lord."

"She must have all the time she might wish."

"Of course, my lord."

Sidley withdrew his cane and dismissed Pinxton with a languid wave of one hand. But Marian was scarcely aware of the clerk's departure. Lord Sidley held her complete attention.

At once she understood Katie's enchantment. He was a tall man, splendidly built, and once again carefully and expensively dressed, without flamboyance or ostentation. His coat was dark—not the black that Colonel Bassett had so heatedly disparaged but a depth of midnight blue. And his hair was dark, and his brows were dark, but his self-satisfied smile was very amused and warm.

"We meet again," he said to her.

The comment reminded Marian of their surroundings and the shop's too-eager audience of patrons. She glanced self-consciously at Sidley's companions—both strangers to her—one very young and fair, with an expression of almost comic affability; the other tall and gaunt, of sober demeanor and rather penetrating light eyes. Marian's gaze sought her maid, who hugged the paint box, her mouth agape. The girl stood stupefied by the steps into the store's central aisle.

Sidley understood her dilemma. Glancing casually about, he signaled young Lord Wilfred, one of Edgar's friends, and Wilfred, looking as though he had been summoned to Olympus, moved with alacrity to the table.

"My-my lord Sidley," he stammered, "Er-Lord Benjamin." He bowed first to the fair young man at Sidley's side, then straightened before bowing to her. "Miss Ware."

Marian had caught an expression on Sidley's face that she attributed to weariness or boredom. She did not like him to look so—not in her presence—and determined to execute the civilities most speedily.

"Lord Wilfred, I should like to thank these gentlemen. If you would do the honors?"

"With pleasure, Miss Ware. Lord Benjamin, Lord Sidley, Lord Vaughn—may I present Miss Ware, cousin to Lord Formsby and his sister, Lady Katherine."

As she curtsied, Marian suspected that the bookseller's shop had never before seen such an elegantly synchronized salutation. She quickly proffered her thanks before Sidley's companions neatly drew Wilfred away.

Sidley fixed his amused gaze upon her. "We meet again," he repeated. Though his look was warm, he did not quite smile. "And over"—he peered at the volume on the table—"*The Microcosm of London*." His instant, backward identification impressed her. " 'Tis beautifully rendered, but I would recommend touring the city's treasures in person. You have not been here long, have you, Miss Ware?"

"Just this fortnight," she said, troubled by her breathlessness. "I am here to study."

"And what do you study?"

"Painting—drawing . . ."

"You are an artist."

Marian might only have imagined the faint query in his voice, but her chin rose all the same. "I am learning, my lord."

Again she read the amusement in his gaze.

"We cannot all be Van Dycks, Miss Ware," he conceded, and this time he did smile. "You must have your family—you must have Lady Formsby take you to Ackermann's on one of their open evenings." Sidley gestured to the book. "You might see these prints as originals."

"I would enjoy that."

"And perhaps, since you are an expert, I might consult you with regard to my own choice of portraitist. 'Tis a pressing matter, I assure you. I am informed I must commemorate myself and otherwise leave my mark. Nollekens shall do my bust"—he made a point of yawning over the selection of such a celebrated, and expensive, sculptor—"but I am distracted by choice with regard to my portrait."

Marian regarded him closely, and with some skepticism. She wondered if he merely made polite conversation; it was beyond belief that he might truly desire her opinion. Surely he had no end of people with whom he could consult. And in her estimation no competent artist could harm him, for aside from an unusual pallor he looked superb.

She thought with some impatience that he no doubt knew very well how he looked—and wished to look more so.

"There is always Mr. Thomas Lawrence—" she began.

"I am not *that* vain, Miss Ware." His gaze, which she noticed was vividly blue, laughed at her, such that she could not prevent the pert thought that he seemed vain enough.

His fine eyebrows arched. "D'you know, Miss Ware, you have such a remarkably expressive face, I believe I might guess at your thoughts." As her color rose, he added, "Though perhaps not. In any event, I have decided against Lawrence. I do not seek embellishment, merely a record."

"You are also a student of the arts, my lord?"

"Indeed, Miss Ware. Though my talent is, alas, simple appreciation. But I am fortunate to possess a family collection of some quality. Perhaps one day you might—pardon me, Lord Formsby might—allow me to introduce you to it." He seemed only then to become conscious of the crowd around them. "How they do gawk," he remarked flatly.

"You have just insured they have something at which to gawk."

Again his laughing gaze turned to her. "You reprove me?"

"My lord, I beg your pardon—"

"Do not apologize. It does not suit you—as it suits Mr. Pinxton." He surveyed the crowd again. "Society is an ill-trained beast, Miss Ware, that must be tugged into line now and then, like a hound upon a leash."

"And you would do the tugging, Lord Sidley?"

He laughed. "I decided some time ago 'twas far better to entertain than to crave entertainment." He tapped his cane lightly upon the floor. "Well, 'tis only an interlude. We are the miracle of the moment, to be supplanted, I assure you, by supper time." And while Marian was reflecting that he, at least, was most unlikely to be supplanted in so short a time, his gaze moved beyond her. "Ah, fair Lady Katherine . . ."

Marian heard the speculation in his voice, and wondered if Sidley had some particular interest in Katie. Certainly his attention focused on her with a measuring regard. For all her cousin's beauty and liveliness, Marian had never once felt envious of her. But, given Sidley's close scrutiny, she was uncomfortably aware that the emotion now threatened. With that disturbing recognition, Marian watched Sidley bow to her cousin.

"I must take my leave, Miss Ware. Do not forget that Pinxton awaits your orders. I suspect he will be most eager to oblige you."

"But"—Marian glanced in some confusion at the open volume—"but what do you wish, my lord?"

"I wish what you wish, Miss Ware," he said, smiling as he held her gaze. Then he was strolling away—how he managed that while hiding a limp, she could not fathom—and was soon lost in the crowd.

"Oh, Marian!" Katie gushed, reaching her and taking her arm. "I could not believe it! You were speaking with *Sidley*!"

"Yes." Though what had passed seemed somewhat more than speaking. "Yes," she repeated without enthusiasm.

"If I did not know you very well, Marian," Katie said slyly, "I might think you very naughty!"

"Do not speak so, Katie. You never used to."

And Katie had the good grace to bite her lip. But she still wanted to know what had been said, which Marian described as mere pleasantries. In all truthfulness, though, she had to acknowledge that Lord Sidley had distinguished Katie by describing her as "fair."

"Really?" Katie asked archly, which Marian found she could not quite like. She had to attribute her cousin's surprise to Sidley's acknowledgment, because Katie had always accepted the fact. Given her pale golden curls, lovely green eyes, and engaging, vivacious manner, she was well used to attention and praise.

Katie had come inside merely to collect Marian, as Hatchards's riches held little to distract her, the more so once she realized that Lord Sidley and his company had left the premises. In any event, Lady Formsby awaited them in the carriage. Marian did remember to let a relieved Mr. Pinxton know that the volume in question would suit Lord Sidley admirably; she had determined that such a book would grace any gentleman's library, and that Sidley should be made to pay for his folly in charging her with a decision.

Katie relayed an enthusiastic report to her mother of Marian's encounter, concluding with the bold claim that she had decided to invite Lord Sidley to her ball.

Lady Formsby ignored the comment and turned her attention to Marian.

"What did you think of him, then, my dear?" she asked. "Have his manners improved? 'Tis unusual that he should have spoken to you, much less tasked a stranger in such a way."

"He is a most . . . curious gentleman."

" 'Curious'?" Katie scoffed. "Surely you cannot mean you find anything to disapprove in him?"

"I am hardly in a position to disapprove of Lord Sidley, Katie. But, no, I believe . . . that there is something rather perplexing about him. And that perhaps . . . well, I believe that perhaps he meant to be kind, Aunt," Marian said, with sudden understanding, though she did not explain.

" 'Kind'?" In the evening dimness inside the carriage Marian could feel Edith's frown. "Did you think he looked well?"

"Well? Oh, yes. Very." She blushed, remembering

how very well he had looked in that fine coat. "He looked very . . . well."

"But did you not notice his pallor, Marian?"

"Indeed, he did look very pale. But I assumed that he must not be outdoors much yet, because of his—his cane. His limp, ma'am." In the resulting silence she sensed something unwelcome. "Do you suggest more, Edith?"

"Without question there is more, Marian, as I have it from his aunt, Lady Adeline, that for the past month Sidley has been treating night as day and involving himself in the most regrettable excesses of dissipation."

"I do not care, Mama," Katie inserted boldly. "I intend to marry him anyway."

"Then you are a gudgeon, Katherine, and must be prepared to wear widow's weeds. For you know as well as I that Lord Sidley is said to be dying."

Chapter Two

"**I** cannot help but believe, Sidley," Lord Benjamin said the next morning, "that what you are doing is rather wicked."

"You should never qualify 'wicked,' Benny."

"What? Oh—I see. Yes. Quite!"

Leland Erasmus Pell, eighth Earl of Sidley, turned from his dressing mirror to smile at his friends. "There is no question I am engaged in a deceit of outstandingly evil proportion. Would you not agree, Vaughn?"

Viscount Vaughn sent him a pointed look. "Agree," he said, and returned to an examination of his immaculately buffed Hessian boots.

"Vaughn would have me claim numerous 'deceits,' Benny," Sidley said as his man gave a final brush to his coat. "My deceits multiply. In for a penny, in for a pound!

But wicked as I may be, you must admit that none of this was at my initiative."

"Certainly not!" Lord Benjamin began to pace about the room. "Your aunt is much to blame. Cutting up rough like that! Carrying on as though you were already in your grave! No one could convince her—But really, Sidley—once having, having submitted to—having let the notion—"

"Having let the lie stand, I might only redeem myself by refuting it?"

"Yes!"

"I intend to do so, my Lord Benjamin. But the execution . . ." Sidley shrugged his shoulders, or as near as he could shrug in the close-fitting coat. "I must play out this hand in the most satisfactory manner."

"You must leave town," Vaughn said firmly. "To die— or recover."

"I think I should prefer to recover, Vaughn," Sidley said with a sidelong glance. "Though it does present the greater difficulty." He smiled. "But by good fortune, I needn't determine my fate just this minute."

"It has gone on far too long," Vaughn said. "You cannot fool everyone indefinitely. You must end it, Sidley." He glanced at the volume lying in its wrapping paper on a side table. "I believe I saw a copy of the *Microcosm* in your library last week."

"So you did."

"Then this one is . . . ?"

"A gift, Vaughn. I shall send it on to Lady Formsby with my compliments."

"To Lady Formsby?"

"Lady Formsby is a very dear friend of my aunt's. And an enthusiast for the latest in printing techniques. Did you not know?"

Vaughn returned to an examination of his boots, but now he was frowning.

Lord Benjamin stopped pacing the floor. "Your aunt, Lady Adeline, knows then, Sidley? That you have never been *that* ill?"

"She knew within the first forty-eight hours, Benny. But by then the damage had been done. And all her subsequent protests were ascribed to a fond relative's wishful thinking." Sidley smiled but shook his head. It still amazed him, how remarkably the tale had spread. The formidable Lady Adeline Pell, that model of composure, collapsing in hysterics. On seeing her nephew, pale and still as a corpse, carried on a litter from the *Lark* at Portsmouth, she had shrieked to all present that he was dying, before succumbing herself to an astonishing fit of the vapors.

Though the combination of illness, inebriation, and severe *mal de mer* had indeed rendered Sidley temporarily insensible, he had in fact been assured at least a few more days of life.

But the gossips had speculated wildly. Once he had rallied enough to attempt correction, no one had believed him. Of course he would deny it, wouldn't he? Such a gentlemanly thing to do, to divert attention from his difficulty. Why, the man could scarcely walk! And similarly, though Lady Adeline had made every conceivable effort to refute the talk—her nephew was not dying; she had been overcome on seeing his distress; he was, after all, the last Sidley—her own reputation for near-stoic reserve had been her undoing. Poor woman, the *ton* had clucked, she was fated to experience a most difficult mourning. It seemed Lady Adeline was destined to wear black for many more years.

Frustrated by such implacable belief, still recovering his health, and unwilling to make public mockery of his aunt, Sidley had ceased to protest. And yielding had brought with it unanticipated benefits and pleasures—for one, an absurd forgiveness of failings, but most noticeably a freedom from both expectation and restriction. Though he was still passably young, titled, comfortably wealthy, and not, he hoped, too physically repugnant, marriage-minded mamas had no wish for their daughters to be too soon widowed.

Or did they? Sidley frowned as he glanced at his friends' reflections in the mirror. Benjamin and Vaughn, however reluctantly, had aided him in furthering his deception. They had also provided invaluable insights into the thinking of the *ton*. Despite Sidley's efforts to remove himself from consideration, to indicate that his finances might be troubled—a lack of the ready which he sought to emphasize with some of his more preposterous wagers—the interest had persisted. Increasingly, the young ladies indicated that they shouldn't much mind a brief marriage—if it were succeeded by a well-funded, and no doubt equally brief, mourning.

Which brought him to his Aunt Adeline's plans. She had, she claimed, unintentionally permitted him this holiday. But she had her hopes for the family, or, more accurately, for its expansion. He might kick over the traces for a time, but she expected him to do his duty, preferably by marrying a young lady of her choosing. And she had recently fixed her hopes on the beautiful and buoyant Lady Katherine, young Lord Formsby's sister.

Sidley sighed.

He had been enjoying his idyll, with its glorious absence of accountability. Though his aunt had accused him of making an exhibition of himself, she could not truly fault him. He had only done what any exhausted and relieved veteran of the years-long Peninsular campaign might reasonably have been expected to do in his first weeks home—and to the same excess. Though he was to some extent limited by his still-game leg, all his other faculties had recovered. Aunt Adeline wanted him to turn his mind to the future—and so he had. Not a day passed that he did not deal with correspondence regarding Aldersham or the other estates, Sidley House, tenants, workmen, or vexations of one sort or another. He knew his romp must shortly end. But Lady Katherine? He did not wish to apply himself to marriage and setting up a nursery. Certainly there could be no reason for hurry.

He was still shy of thirty. He was not, after all, fading any more precipitously than the next man.

"If Lady Adeline knows," Lord Benjamin mused aloud, having taken again to pacing, "why won't she *convince* everyone?"

"She has tried, Benny," Sidley said, "but the mob will not budge. Once having placed me on my last legs, society is equally determined to topple me into my grave. I shall probably have fathered my third child before all of them awake to the reality."

"You intend to be a father, then?" Vaughn asked.

Sidley sent his friend a guarded look. Vaughn had ever been too perceptive. "Not imminently. I should hardly have troubled to go to such lengths to evade the matchmakers if I were eager to deliver up an heir."

"Then why your pronounced interest in Miss Ware?"

"'Pronounced'? I assure you, I have no interest in Miss Ware."

"You stared at her for fully twenty minutes at the Osbornes' rout last week."

"Did I? I was unaware of it. As was she."

"Why'd you intervene yesterday evening, then?" Benny asked.

"Because the young lady was at a disadvantage. I believe only *I* should place people at a disadvantage."

Benny grinned but pressed, "And you played the gallant that first time as well—because she was at a disadvantage?"

"Perhaps I needn't 'play,' you young cub. Perhaps Miss

Ware inspires gallantry. But you forget—she had her cousin Formsby as escort. You may have observed that he lacks a certain care. Miss Ware might easily have suffered a fall. Indeed, Formsby is so shortsighted, he sees little beyond his lapels." Sidley pointedly brushed his own lapels.

"How I admire you, Sidley!" Lord Benjamin gushed. "To be in town mere weeks, and all the crack! New, and unknown, and unlikely to last! 'Tis such a coup! My word, I am in awe!"

Sidley shook his head at Benny's raptures. He and Vaughn had taken the younger man in hand as a favor to Benjamin's father, the Duke of Derwin. His Grace, fearing that his third son's enthusiasms might otherwise lead the boy into more mischief than the scamp had already sampled, had pressed an oversight role upon the two older men.

"Before you commend him too thoroughly, Benny," Vaughn cautioned, "let us see how he extricates himself from this business."

"You doubt that I shall?" Sidley asked.

"Confessing to such a clanker will be hard enough—without the added difficulty."

" 'Added difficulty'?"

"You are in very grave danger, my friend."

"*Grave* danger, hah!" Benny laughed. "I like that!"

But Sidley was not to be diverted. "Explain yourself, Vaughn," he said sharply.

"Miss Ware."

"Miss Ware is in no danger. I do not trifle with young ladies'—"

"'Tis *your* danger I mentioned, not hers."

"What's this, then?" Benny asked. "Isn't Miss Ware just a bit of a sparrow?"

As Sidley's glance narrowed on Benny, Vaughn laughed. "You lack discernment, Benny," he said. "The girl is lovely."

"Undoubtedly," Sidley agreed. "Since your taste runs to painted opera dancers, Benny, or—to stretch your metaphor—to flamingos, Miss Ware's subtler attractions must elude you. I myself should most liken her to—oh, a thrush, perhaps. Or a nightingale." He did not look at his friends as he dabbed more powder onto his face. "Never forget that paint tends to mask more than it reveals, young Benny"—he turned at last from his mirror—"and that a gown tends to reveal more than any woman suspects we see."

As Benny laughed again, Vaughn snorted. "You look even more ashen than you did yesterday."

"That is the aim, my friend."

"But since you will be recovering . . . ?"

"Not yet."

"You will not long be able to hide your own health, Lee. You bested Hewitt yesterday morning at Jackson's."

"But I have not yet bested you, Vaughn."

"I would take out your leg."

"No one else would dare. So you see, I am not fit enough."

Benny was again pacing with his annoyingly youthful energy. "Miss Ware, a thrush?" he repeated. "Yes, I see it. She is pretty enough, I 'spose, if viewed apart from her cousin, Lady K. Else she wouldn't be betrothed."

Sidley checked himself in the act of pulling on his gloves. "Miss Ware is betrothed?" he asked lightly. "To whom?"

"Does it matter?" Vaughn asked.

"Oh, some naval lieutenant," Benny supplied. "From her home in Northants. Apparently a friend of her brother, the curate. We had it from Wilfred last night."

"And why did you not tell me this last night?"

"Does it matter?" Vaughn repeated.

"Why," Benny responded, "we was travelin' on to Brooks's, and it completely slipped my mind. I—"

" 'Tis nothing," Sidley said quickly, turning to examine his collar closely in the mirror. He concentrated with some effort. "Where is this naval lieutenant?"

"Where would you wish him, Sidley?" Vaughn asked. "The bottom of the sea? He is due back from Gibraltar within the month."

Sidley felt as though a much-anticipated meal had just been removed from in front of his nose. The reaction surprised him; perhaps Vaughn was right, and he really had been in some danger. He would not have credited it, on such short acquaintance.

He forced himself to smile at Vaughn as he accepted his cane from his valet. "Then there is no problem, my friend. Since I now know Miss Ware to be doomed to the altar, and she believes me simply doomed, we are admirably matched. What harm in that, Vaughn?" And, reflecting that he was a bigger fraud even than his friends supposed, he escorted them from his dressing room.

"Whatever can he mean by it?" Katie wailed, the brown paper wrapping slipping from her lap onto the floor. "Sending Mama a *book*?"

Marian gazed at Katie's pretty, puzzled face, then reached across to rescue the volume before it, too, slid to the carpet. " 'Tis a beautiful book, Katie."

" 'Beautiful'! Marian, are you daft? How can a book be beautiful?" Katie fussed with the wrapping before setting it aside in an ungainly bundle. "Perhaps there truly is something wrong with Lord Sidley. In . . . in an eccentric way, you understand. And it is a shame, too, for he is so very handsome. And I do think he dresses divinely. But I am not at all certain I should find it agreeable, tolerating some of these pranks he plays."

"Sending a gift of a book is scarcely a prank."

"*You* may not think it so, Marian, for you like the dusty old things. Why could he not send flowers—or some sweets—as all the other gentlemen do?"

"I suspect that is the last thing Lord Sidley should ever want—" Marian said, staring thoughtfully out the window at the bright afternoon, "—to be like all the other gentlemen."

She had spent most of the morning painting in Edith's charming walled garden, where the late-spring and early-summer blooms warred for prominence. Despite the auspicious weather, Marian had been unable to shake her melancholy. Her thoughts had dwelt overmuch on one subject.

Lord Sidley's sad prospects depressed her. And she felt crushed, some part of her grieved, that Katie disparaged this magnificent book, which had been forwarded so kindly. Bestowing it might even have been his last act.

Marian ran her fingers lightly over the binding, then opened the book. Her aunt had mistakenly assumed the offering for Katie, but Marian thought that most unlikely. She was convinced that the *Microcosm* had been intended for her. And now she must thank the sender, though she did not know how. She feared to look again into those laughing eyes and find herself near tears.

At twenty, she had had too much of death. The passing of her mother and, four years later, her father, had left her an orphan at sixteen. Her village had lost many men to decades of war, and for two years Marian had feared for William Reeves's safety on the high seas. She would not have wanted to believe herself callous to any life, but her dismay at the thought of Lord Sidley's end confounded her. She could not attribute her concern to solicitude for Katie, because Katie seemed remarkably sanguine regarding her favorite's fate. So Marian had concluded that she must simply *like* Lord Sidley, as strange and inexplicable as that thought might be. Because she hardly knew him and apparently never would.

" 'Twas a kindness to send this, Katie," she repeated. "The illustrations are astonishing. You shall see. When you are away from town, you will treasure this as a remembrance."

Katie grinned roguishly. "I intend to return to town often enough never to *need* a remembrance, Marian. But you are so sweet to make the best of this. Perhaps you ought to keep the book, for when you return to Brinford. You are unlikely to return to town very often once you are wed."

That was certainly true. William had always claimed to dislike London. And he had written often enough in his letters that he had seen his fill of the world. Upon his return he intended to purchase a holding near Brinford and never leave. Though she loved Northamptonshire, Marian found that limited a future difficult to contemplate.

Her fingers trembled against the pages. "We must ask your mother," she said. "Perhaps she will want it for the country—for Enderby."

"Oh, Mama never looks at half the books she buys! Do keep it, Marian. I am convinced you must appreciate it more than any of us, since you know so much about art."

"Thank you, Katie." Her cousin's consideration, though often carelessly expressed, had always been frequent enough to sustain Marian's own fondness. "Katie, Lord Sidley mentioned that Ackermann's holds an open night each week, for people to view these prints. I am not certain, but I . . . I had the impression that he might try to attend. If we were to go, you might see him there."

"And then I might mention my ball to him in person! Oh, Marian, how shrewd you are! Why, of course we shall go! Unless—Well, let us hope it is not tomorrow. There is Lady Malvern's supper! Let me just see . . ." And she impatiently rang the bell, to ask Jenks to inquire regarding Ackermann's open evening.

Marian cradled the book and wondered why she should find it so disastrously affecting that Lord Sidley should be dying, when Katie, who professed to want to marry the man, should be affected not at all. If Marian were proved correct, and the earl did trouble to grace the Ackermann's showing, she sensed it would be in her best interest to leave him to Katie's company. If she were to speak to him, she might embarrass herself, and he might—what? Tease her? Yet she must thank him.

She thought of feigning illness and letting Katie go alone to Ackermann's. But Marian had rarely been ill a day in her life. And given Sidley's situation, the ploy seemed grossly unacceptable, even craven. She could only do her best to avoid him.

That resolve was more easily kept in the abstract. For when she and her cousins entered Ackermann's three nights later for the weekly viewing, Marian's sole wish was for Lord Sidley's presence. She did not spot him on entering and moved about listlessly before stopping to examine closely a stunning, printed depiction of a fire in London.

"You were not there," Lord Sidley said very softly. Though he stood at her side, he looked not at her but at the print before them. At her quizzical silence he explained, "You did not attend Lady Malvern's supper."

"I was not expected to attend."

"*I* expected you." As he turned to her, one of his dark eyebrows rose. "You are more selective than your cousin?"

"I am not—" Marian looked away from his surprisingly accusing gaze. "I have not been presented at court, my lord. I am here only for the month, and only to study, not to seek—not to seek companionship."

"You are still one of the family, and should be welcome in society. Though you may not indeed be seeking companionship, as you so subtly term it. I understand you have already sniggled a fellow. I commend you, Miss Ware. When is the happy day?"

She did not like the word *sniggled* any more than she cared for his tone of voice. "Lieutenant Reeves and I—"

"You call him 'Lieutenant,' then?"

"Of course not. William is—"

"Ah, *William*!"

Marian looked him full in the face. "You sound rather unpleasant, my lord."

" 'Sound'? Miss Ware, I had no inkling that my voice offended."

" 'Tis not your voice. 'Tis your tone."

"Well, with regard to tone, I know enough of music—"

"My lord, I will not spar with you."

"I regret that very much."

She reviewed him then—his magnificent, bottle green coat, his high shirt points, and his delicately crafted cravat. His elegant dress distracted from his too-pale complexion. But his manner, his nonchalance, distressed her. And for some unfathomable reason she felt extremely angry.

"I suppose," Marian said softly, as quietly as she could, "I suppose we must all indulge you, Lord Sidley, because you are . . . because of your disappointed prospects. The rest of us must bear with your ill humors, and suffer your deficits in courtesy, because the sad truth is that we need not suffer them for long."

He answered her with silence. Marian wished instantly to take back the words. She kept her attention fixed on the print before her while she struggled to think. She should have thought before. But she was not given the opportunity to recover.

"Apparently you've been apprised of my impending demise. Nothing else might so easily explain the alteration in your manner. Though I confess, I must indeed have been indulged by others, since I am more used to sympathy than scorn. Your own *tone,* Miss Ware, is quite scathing."

She turned quickly to face him. "My lord, please permit me to apologize. I could not be more sorry, and as for sympathy—"

"Spare me, Miss Ware. On such short acquaintance, your sympathy can only be perfunctory."

Marian drew a sharp breath. "Even strangers," she managed, "like myself, might . . . might feel for you, my lord."

" 'Feel for' me? How quaint. I assure you, there is little feeling involved, merely curiosity, that of watching my morbidly entertaining little existence come to its close."

He observed her narrowly; she thought she must look as ill as she felt.

"Do not waste your time pitying me, Miss Ware. You are young, with much to experience and enjoy yet in life. Indeed, anticipating your marriage! What can I be to you?" He did not give her a chance to attempt an answer, but shrugged and again looked away. "And perhaps my situation is not as dire as others would have it. In fact, I might wager so. I choose to be optimistic. However inconvenient you might find it that I should linger, or even survive." His smile when he turned back to her was humorless.

Marian knew she was blushing; she could do nothing for it. And, sharp as he sounded, Lord Sidley seemed to derive satisfaction from toying with her.

"Our conversation has been so diverting, Miss Ware, that I find I still await the answer to my question. When do you and Lieutenant William Reeves wed?"

"Perhaps later this summer. We have not yet determined. We are friends of many years. . . ."

"How delightful! There is nothing like a carefully measured romance to warm one's blood. One would never wish an excess of anticipation to spoil the nuptials."

"That is an unconscionably suggestive—" Marian broke off and bit her lip. "No doubt you, my lord, have great contempt for delay and yield frequently to the madness of the moment—"

" 'Frequently'!"

"—and would have no understanding of arrangements that extend beyond the immediately available."

His eyebrows shot up. "My word! What has put you in such a pother? Surely I am to be permitted a few excesses. My time may be limited. And duty has not been so kind to me that I'm now inclined to neglect my pleasures. Forgive me. I would not in the usual way speak so to a young lady, Miss Ware, but you do . . . provoke me."

Marian looked down and swallowed. "It is no concern of mine, of course. Do you—have you—that is, my cousin Katie—"

"Lady Katherine is charming!"

"Yes, she is," Marian said, meeting his gaze once more. "And she thinks most highly of *you,* my lord."

"I am glad to hear it," he accepted lazily.

"I should not like to see her hurt."

"No indeed!" He peered down his nose at her. "Has someone hurt her?"

"Oh! You are—Of course I am concerned that *you* should not hurt her!"

"I believe I might safely claim that I shan't." He frowned at her. "On Saturday, at the Malverns', Lady

Katherine invited me to this week's ball. No doubt you know that."

"You must not feel pressured to attend on such short notice . . ."

"Do you not wish me to attend, Miss Ware?"

"Why, of course it is nothing to do with me. But Katie would be most disappointed."

He was again examining her face. "Did you receive the book, Miss Ware?"

"Oh! Oh, yes indeed. It was so very thoughtful . . . and we are all most, most appreciative."

" 'All' of you?" His lips twitched, but his gaze was serious. "Miss Ware, we have not done well here this evening. The fault rests entirely with me. Might we start again?"

He spoke softly, confidingly. The request was generous. In that instant Marian sensed her heart was very much at risk. But she had not even a second to reflect on the discovery.

"There you are!" Katie said at her side. "Has Lord Sidley been entertaining you, Marian?"

"Miss Ware has been most forbearing," Sidley offered. "I fear I have grown tiresome."

"Not at all, my lord," Marian managed. "I look forward to continuing our discussion at some future date."

"Perhaps at Lady Katherine's ball?" he asked, and his gaze met hers steadily as Katie tapped his arm with her fan.

"You have decided to attend, my lord!"

"With great pleasure, Lady Katherine. Miss Ware." And he bowed before departing.

"Oh, I knew he would!" Katie enthused. "He was most coy last night—he even claimed he might have another engagement—but now here he is, obliging as can be. I do hope I shan't have much difficulty with him."

" 'Difficulty'?" Marian had some trouble swallowing the lump in her throat.

"Why, if we are to be married, I should hope for a good deal more amiability. Complaisance."

Complaisance! From Lord Sidley? Marian glanced at her cousin with some impatience. "I wonder, Katie, if you understand the man at all."

"Oh, do not sound so severe, Marian. Honestly, just because you yourself are engaged, 'tis no reason to assume you know everything about gentlemen."

"That is not what I assume! I spoke only of Lord Sidley."

"And why should you know Lord Sidley better than I?"

Marian could summon no response. She knew only that Katie's plans and attitude filled her with something akin to foreboding.

"No reason at all, Katie," she said at last. "You are right—I am imagining much. You know it is always my way."

And with that disclaimer Katie seemed thankfully content.

Chapter Three

"Lady Katherine would do very well for you, Sidley." His aunt, Adeline, regally ensconced in a high-backed chair, smoothed out her black bombazine skirt. She had worn mourning for her brother, Sidley's father, and now wore mourning for her nephew, Sidley's brother. Indeed, when Sidley reflected upon it, Lady Adeline Pell had worn mourning of some sort for the greater part of the past thirty years. "Edgar, Lord Formsby, has already declined several offers for his sister's hand," she added. "The girl is of excellent family, an admired beauty, just bearably loud, and shall have at least four thousand a year."

Sidley turned fully from the window, from which he'd been pensively observing the street outside the family's town home. "And you believe those qualities are what should suit me?"

"They are qualities that should suit any gentleman in your position."

"What a boon to matchmaking, that all of us should be so conveniently interchangeable."

"This is a serious matter, Sidley. Your quirky humors are ill-gauged to the matter of matrimony. I was half-afraid you would return home wed to a Spanish dancer!"

"Were you?" He smiled. "Instead, I gave you a different kind of fright."

"Yes, well, we will speak no more of that," she said uncomfortably. Her loss of composure on his return would forever be a source of embarrassment for her. "You are well enough now, and equally well cognizant of your duty."

"Yes," Sidley said on a sigh, at last abandoning the window to take a seat at the fire, across from his aunt. He selected a sweet of some sort from the tea tray between them and tossed it indifferently into his mouth. For the past few days he had lacked appetite, but he knew he must continue to build his strength. He looked steadily across at his aunt, of whom he was surpassingly fond, despite her tendency to management.

"So, pretty and pampered Lady Katherine meets with your approval, does she? You are certain your friendship with her mother has not swayed you too positively? The girl is very young."

"Eighteen is a perfect age! And why should I not be 'swayed positively,' as you say, by as close a friend as the Countess of Formsby? Edith and I have always understood each other."

"Did you plot this fate at the foot of Lady Katherine's cradle then, Auntie? Or—I had forgotten—no doubt she was intended for m'brother Simon, who, by the way, would almost have been old enough to be the chit's father."

"Not quite, Sidley," Lady Adeline corrected him. "And in your case, a difference of ten or eleven years will scarcely signify."

"More than a decade is a great deal of experience."

"In my opinion, some of your more recent *experiences* would have been better avoided."

"I see you wish my brief holiday to end."

"It has not been that brief."

"I beg to differ. Six weeks is nothing at all." He sat back on the sofa and idly tapped his left boot with his cane. "And I have not been wholly well. You think me a more attractive prospect than I am, Aunt Adeline."

"Humbug! You are the prize catch of the season, even given the . . . the . . ."

"My imminent death? I believe my numbered days are precisely what has propelled me to the top of the ladies' lists."

"Do not be coarse, Lee. You were always considered a prize. Even as a second son."

"Really! Why?"

"I shall not flatter you, outrageous boy." Adeline sniffed delicately as she eyed him. "You always had funds enough through your mother."

"No doubt you have the right of it, Auntie. My personal charms have never mattered in the slightest." But his smile faded as he looked again to the fire. "Simon should have stayed at home and seen to the family fortunes. We would have been spared much."

"We could no more keep him at home than we could keep you. After Vitoria he was wild to go."

"The more fool he," Sidley muttered darkly. "After Vitoria I wanted only to return. But I digress. You wish me married and starting a nursery. Re-establishing the eroded Sidley line! I intend to do as I must. As you say, there is considerable property at stake. But next season strikes me as sufficiently soon."

His aunt shook her head. "You will be twenty-nine this December."

"Surely that is not too ancient, ma'am?"

"To assure the line, you need an heir."

"There is an heir," Sidley countered impatiently. "Cousin Nigel shall do nicely."

"Nigel Boscombe is a fool!"

"As I said, he shall do nicely."

"You cannot convince me you are pleased that Nigel might inherit."

"I am not pleased. You know very well how thoroughly the prospect repels me. Not enough, however, to suffer the lifelong irritation of rushing to prevent it." He fingered the sofa's upholstery. "I should prefer to hold out for some soupçon of affection."

" 'Soupçon of affection'! Would you even recognize it, I wonder?"

His gaze measured her. "I should recognize it, Auntie," he said softly. He looked again to the fire. "I am fully aware that if I am to secure my own interests, I must necessarily look to the interests of others. Every day I receive correspondence relating to some pressing problem or another. Too much has been ignored for too long. Though you think me carelessly oblivious, I must stress that, under the circumstances, troubling to pursue my more personal desires assumes the nature of a challenge. I am working hard at enjoying life, ma'am."

"My dear," she began, "I am not recommending that you abandon any thought of eventually building some rapport, some affection, with a wife. After all, your parents were most famously enamored."

"If my parents' marriage is to be upheld as an example, I am not at all certain I should choose to emulate it. Do you think Father would have repeated it?"

"My brother loved your mother, Lee. He bore with so much *because* he loved her. He would have wanted to wed if only for a day."

Sidley looked at her skeptically. "Father was never that much of a simpleton."

"Indeed he was—about Alicia, and at age twenty-five."

"And who is to say I shan't have Mother's problems?"

"Alicia showed certain . . . erratic behaviors even in

her teens, though none of us understood them for what they were. Mercifully, neither Simon nor you ever exhibited the same. You cannot on any rational basis believe in the likelihood."

"Those who might have me must consider it."

"I have not heard mention of any perceived taint. And I assure you, I keep abreast of the talk."

Sidley smiled at his aunt's claim. "I would never question *that,* ma'am." Again he tapped his cane against his boot and considered the fire. "Speaking of the talk, have you heard anything of Miss Ware, Lady Katherine's cousin?"

"You expect me to know everyone, do you?" she asked.

"Perhaps because you *do* seem to know everyone, Auntie. Even cousins."

"Have you met her, then? Edith has not yet brought Miss Ware 'round to call. I believe tutorials of some sort pose an impediment, absorbing the girl's time. Miss Ware is the daughter of Edith's first cousin, of whom she was particularly fond. The mother tossed away her portion to run off and marry a soldier—an educated man, and respectable, but not up to the Satterthwaite family standards. I do not recall much of the history, but Miss Ware and her brother were left orphans some four or five years ago, when the father passed. The brother is a curate in Northamptonshire, with expectations of a living in the near term. He intends to wed this fall. Edith has much affection for Marian Ware. She claims the girl is a most positive influence on Lady Katherine. I believe Miss Ware's in town just this June, studying—oh, something."

"Art," he supplied. "She is a painter."

His aunt's gaze settled disconcertingly on his. "Is she?" she asked.

"So she says. I've not seen the evidence. But she has hinted at the knowledge—and the temperament."

"Has she?"

This time Sidley looked to the fire. "She must be some years older than Lady Katherine," he said. "She has greater composure. But they seem most companionable."

"So I understood—from Edith." There was a moment's pause; then she asked sharply, "What are you about?"

He turned in amusement to his aunt's stern gaze. "Do not panic, my dear," he assured her. "Miss Ware is affianced, as you no doubt know, and due to wed this summer. I mention her only because it occurred to me that she would be good company—for Lady Katherine, of course—at your proposed house party. I should advise including her in your invitation."

"You intend to join me at Aldersham next week, then?"

"I think I must, as you have troubled to invite such scintillating and outstandingly *eligible* company. Amusements here in town grow tedious. We have had our fill of celebrations and rude foreign princes. Everyone talks only of the country. Vaughn and Benjamin and I had planned a country spree in any event."

"I do not like 'sprees,' Sidley. There will be no all-night carousing at Aldersham. This is a most serious business."

"But we cannot alert our guests to that, surely? All must be joyful entertainment. I must not be perceived as *seeking,* and the young ladies must not be displayed as the *sought.* We shall be delightfully obtuse. And rather falsely *intime.* I take it you have selected some additional candidates for me, should young Lord Formsby find reason to reject my offer, or Lady Katherine decline to wed a corpse?"

"I wish you would not speak so," his aunt reproved. "And at Aldersham, you must be seen to improve in health—away from town's dissipations."

"The country's dissipations might replace them."

"I shall not countenance it, Sidley! You forget that Aldersham is my home, for the rest of my days."

He laughed. "I do not forget it, ma'am. Indeed, how could I forget it? I merely tease you. I shall be on my best behavior and squire whomever you wish about the garden paths. But I cannot promise you an engagement at the end of the week."

"I shall work on that, you young jackanapes!"

"No doubt." Sidley rose to take his leave. "But do not forget Miss Ware." And he noticed his aunt's frown as he leaned to kiss her good-bye.

Lady Katherine's ball was a squeeze—so well attended, in fact, that had poor weather trapped all the guests inside, there would scarcely have been room for dancing. Fortunately, the wide French doors to the garden were open, there was a breeze, and enough people shifted about to make such movements possible.

The event was one of the last of the season, and a certain sentiment—or relief—appeared to lend heightened gaiety to the gathering. Like a star at its brightest before its end, society flaunted its excesses. Never had the ladies dressed as beautifully; never had the gentlemen strolled as proudly.

Lord Sidley and his fellows, just announced, stood inside the front hall and eyed the glittering crowd.

"This is hard of you, Sidley," Lord Benjamin complained, "forcing me to this."

"'Twill do you no harm, Benny, to spend one evening in respectable company."

"And how would *you* know that?" he countered disagreeably.

Sidley surveyed the youngster carefully through a quizzing glass. He thought the cub ill-mannered enough to deserve a set-down. But he reminded himself of his promise to Derwin. And he did not want any upset this evening. As his gaze left Benny to wander over the ballroom, he at last found Lady Formsby—and then Marian Ware. He did not trouble to locate Lady Katherine. As he turned again to Benny, he forced himself to laugh.

"You are right, of course, my wayward friend. Respectable company and I have recently been strangers.

So, shall we experiment together, just for this one evening?"

To his relief, Benny grinned. "I 'spose one evening is little enough."

"We shan't stay long, Benny," Vaughn added. "Since Sidley cannot dance, and you will not."

"And you, Vaughn," Sidley said, nodding his head toward a couple at the far side of the room, "perhaps should not." He had noticed Griffin Knox and his wife standing in a far corner. Knox, florid-faced and heavy-shouldered, looked what he was—a man who had fought his way to riches and success so single-mindedly that some wags dared call him "Gruff'un" Knox behind his back. He had bought himself a place in society. He had also bought himself a young and pretty wife. It was Vaughn's ill fortune that the spouse Knox had chosen to acquire was Jenny Lanning. When Vaughn had gone to war four years earlier, fair Jenny had been his own intended.

"I am over it, Sidley," Vaughn said softly.

"Good. Then Knox has no cause to make trouble?"

"None at all."

"You have not seen her?"

"I—" Vaughn stopped and stared hard at Lord Benjamin. "Benny will tell you in any event. We encountered Mrs. Knox in Berkeley Square last week. She was passably civil, as was I. There is nothing, Sidley."

"I've never seen a woman look so shattered, Sidley," Benny said. "Shied like a pony. As if she'd seen a ghost."

"A ghost to her, certainly," Vaughn commented. "May I beg the two of you to abandon this subject?"

"He can't be the best of husbands," Benny persisted. "Why, I've seen Knox at some of the worst—"

"Few of us make good husbands," Sidley inserted quickly.

"Perhaps Mrs. Knox does not deserve a good husband," Vaughn said.

Sidley sighed. "You do not believe that, Vaughn," he said, forcing a smile. "We shall dodge them both. There are enough here this evening to make avoidance not only desirable but possible. Let us to it, gentlemen." And he led his companions across the room toward their hostess.

"Lord Sidley has come," Edith said softly at Marian's side. "Late enough to make an entrance, but not so late as to be discourteous."

"I cannot believe he is that calculating, Aunt," Marian said, though she was beginning to have her doubts.

"Can you not, Marian? He is a frightfully intelligent man, and perhaps," she mused aloud, "not best suited for Katie."

"Has he—has he offered, then, Edith?" Marian asked, watching Sidley and his companions begin a slow but impressively received advance around the packed room. Without exception the ladies greeted him rapturously; the men seemed equally divided between delight and awe. Marian's own interest was infinitely more than polite.

"He has not offered, Marian. I begin to hope that he will not. Katie is so set on it—as though to prove that she can bring him up to scratch. Such thinking is not a sound basis for marriage. And given his reported ill health, I am most uneasy. But she will not listen."

"I have my doubts as well, Aunt. Perhaps Lord Sidley suspects the same, for I have not observed any particular preference on his part."

"Haven't you, Marian? There is the matter of the book." When Marian stayed silent, Edith added, "His aunt, Lady Adeline, seems to wish it. I have not had the heart to discourage her. Adeline has had so many disappointments. Oh, look, Marian," she diverted, "Katie dances well with Mr. Merrick."

For a second Marian was distracted, watching her cousin step about gracefully with an obviously enraptured partner.

"Is . . . is Lady Adeline resigned to Lord Sidley's passing then, Aunt?"

"Adeline Pell has never resigned herself to much of anything, Marian. If there is the slightest hope for him, she will admit of no other possibility. But you will see for yourself. I shall take you to meet her on Monday. She sent a note 'round. I believe she wishes you to accompany us to Aldersham."

"Aldersham! But I could not possibly go! I have my work, and—"

"Good heavens, Marian! How can that possibly compare with a visit to Aldersham?"

"Did I hear Aldersham mentioned?" Sidley asked, coming up to them. He bowed low first to Lady Formsby, then to Marian. "It is a place with which I claim some acquaintance."

"Less than you should, so I hear," Lady Formsby said lightly.

"If I were to have your company there, my lady, I should never quit the place."

As her sensible cousin Edith visibly melted, Marian met Sidley's gaze. She knew the danger of holding his very blue attention, but the opportunity was irresistible.

"'Twas most kind of you to come this evening, my lord," she said.

"I should have felt the lack had I not come, Miss Ware." He at last looked away from her to present his companions to her aunt.

"You see my daughter on the floor, Lord Sidley," Lady Formsby said, "but I believe she has held a dance for you this evening."

"That was most kind of her. But, alas, I am not yet agile enough to dance. Perhaps one of my friends would be honored?"

Both Lord Benjamin and Lord Vaughn promptly sought the dance, and Lady Formsby left the decision to Katherine. As his fellows excused themselves to acknowledge others of their acquaintance, Lord Sidley again looked to Marian.

"You are not dancing, Miss Ware."

"I have been, my lord. I merely take a rest."

"Then you must consider showing me some part of the gardens. I would welcome a turn in the air."

You have just arrived, Marian challenged him silently, and she suspected that he had read her thoughts when he claimed, "Air is good for me."

"Certainly, my lord," Edith acknowledged quickly. "Marian, do accompany Lord Sidley outside. There's a good girl."

Inwardly rebelling that she should be so commanded, Marian led the way through the crowd, heedless of whether Lord Sidley followed her or not. But she knew without question that he did. She had thought she looked well this evening—she had caught some glances earlier in her new, beribboned gown—but the attention had been nothing at all like that drawn in advance of Lord Sidley. As the wake of onlookers parted before them, Marian likened herself to the prow of some magnificent, stately vessel.

When they crossed the threshold to the terrace, Marian whirled about—and collided with his chest. "Oh, I do beg your pardon."

"'Tis nothing, Miss Ware." His gaze once again laughed at her. "I am not so easily felled."

No, she thought, glancing at his broad shoulders in his immaculately elegant dark coat, *clearly not.* But his outward solidity reminded her of the transience she would have preferred to forget. As she walked beside him to the stone baluster at the terrace edge, Marian noticed that the earlier crowd of revelers had thinned, no doubt in eager flight to the supper room.

"How do you . . . how do you feel, my lord?" she ventured.

"Exhilarated!"

Marian frowned as she turned to him. "You are jesting."

"Not at all." He gazed about at the softly moonlit gardens. "It is a beautiful evening, and I am in superior company." His glance settled briefly on her face before he glanced up at the windows and balconies of the Formsby town house. "I believe the former Lord Formsby had a great deal of work done to this house. For some prolonged period the entire street was barred to traffic. But that was many years ago."

"Oh, but I recall it. One could not visit without risking a dusting of plaster powder!"

"Perhaps our paths crossed, then."

"I should have remembered."

He considered her warmly. "I was a most unpromising youth, Miss Ware, and decidedly inattentive. No matter how observant a youngster *you* might have been—and I suspect you were very—I cannot vouch for my own recollection. And lately," he mused, looking once again to the well-lit building, "I have become too selective with my few memories."

"Naturally, you must reflect—you must reminisce as you—as you confront such a drastic—"

"I wish you would not refer to my state so, Miss Ware,"

he interrupted. " 'Tis most unsettling. I should prefer you to act as though you know nothing of it."

"I . . . cannot."

A couple passing on the garden path a level below them laughed aloud, in sharp contrast to their own strained mood. Eager for a diversion, Marian reached to touch Sidley's cane, which he had propped against the stonework between them. The cane's tooled silver handle was exquisite.

"This is lovely," she said.

"Yet 'tis flimsy enough," he said, smiling once more. "When one lacks use of a leg, one grasps at straws."

"You have not appeared to need—that is, I have seen you walk without its support."

"I test myself, Miss Ware. But I have yet to brave the absence of its balance. You needn't believe me overly fond of an accessory."

She glanced down, lest he see that was indeed what she had thought, and asked, "The wood is . . . ?"

"Malacca. Does it not sound exotic? In this cane's company I think of Malaya and the distant straits, a place I should dearly love to visit. Imagine it, Miss Ware—lush palms and mangroves by a sea of jade, breezes scented with spices wafting from the islands of Sumatra and Java—But perhaps you shall journey to see as much. With your naval officer."

"That is most unlikely, my lord. Will—Lieutenant Reeves—has written that he is eager for home—to settle in Northampton."

"And that shall satisfy you, then?"

Marian's chin rose. "I love my home."

"In that you are hardly unique. But surely you have some desire to see something of the world, to explore? You would not be here in town if that were not the case."

"It is quite different. In my work I find exploration enough."

Sidley smiled slightly. "Let us hope you shall always be lucky enough to think so." Again he turned to examine the Formsby house façade, so contemplatively that Marian was surprised by his next question.

"How does he fare, then, your lieutenant? He returns soon?"

"I cannot say. I have not heard from him since before I left for town. He is in Gibraltar."

"And mail from Gibraltar often goes astray."

"You would make him inattentive."

"Yes."

"But he is not! He has been most conscientious."

"A fine thing in an officer, Miss Ware. But I've not seen this in the romantic literature—sonnets to the conscientious."

"We are not—that is, we have known each other many years. William is my brother's closest friend. In many ways he is like another brother."

"A husband is not a brother." At her gasp, he said, "Presumably he bested several others there in Northants for your hand—some slack-jawed swains hovering at your doorstep?"

Marian straightened from the balustrade. "Is there a reason," she asked coldly, "you believe any beaux of mine must be 'slack-jawed,' my lord?"

"Why, naturally they would be in awe of both your beauty and your talent."

"You know nothing of my talent."

"I deduce it, Miss Ware. It must rival your beauty, which is considerable." He bowed.

"You needn't flatter me, my lord. There is no one to hear."

"The only one who matters is here."

She thought he leaned closer to her. "It is wrong for you to speak to me so. You must respect my—respect Lieutenant Reeves."

Sidley shrugged. "We have discussed him. I acknowledge his claim. But the man is not present," he said softly, "and that is his misfortune."

Marian could look straight up into his eyes. The bright moonlight robbed them of color but not of depth or darkness. She wondered at herself, to be considering him so minutely, as though he were a subject she intended to paint. But her consciousness was of something else entirely—that of warmth, and closeness, and a much too attractive temptation.

She swallowed and forced herself to break the gaze. She looked to his nose and cheeks—and frowned. He had to be wearing powder, for the moonlight to reflect so little upon his skin.

"Do not peer at me so, Miss Ware. I am too shy for it."

"Shy! Your reputation is otherwise."

"Perhaps I do not deserve my reputation." He smiled and turned his head to listen to a lone flutist playing within the ballroom. "Orpheus is practicing. 'Tis a pleasant tune. I think we might practice as well. Come, Miss Ware, you must help me exercise. Try some simple steps with me. I saw Colonel Bassett dancing as I came in. Even in my decrepit condition I ought to execute a turn as well as old Bassett."

He moved away from the stone rail and extended a gloved hand to her. The flutist's tune, from an old, simple minuet, carried sweetly through the open doors.

"People will see," Marian said, even as she compliantly extended a hand.

"We do not care," he countered. For a moment his smile broadened. "You have such a short time here, Miss Ware. Will you not enjoy it?" His coaxing tone robbed her of any objection, though she did wonder whether he referred to her stay in London or on Earth.

For a minute they stepped slowly and carefully to the melody. When the instrument stopped, they stopped as well, and Marian held her breath as Sidley merely stood and smiled at her. In that brief pause she was conscious of a small audience, but, just as Sidley had claimed, she did not care. As she held his gaze she knew her heart kept pace with the vanished tune. When the flutist resumed, the music did not continue but began again, and Sidley dutifully positioned himself to lead her through a repeat of the initial steps. But beyond those first moves,

as the music advanced to a more intricate passage, he
tried to pivot on his bad leg at a turn, and stumbled.

"Curses . . ." he muttered, gritting his teeth in obvious pain.

"You have done very well."

His bright gaze was sharp. "You speak to me as though
I were twelve."

"I speak to you," she said evenly, "as though you have
been injured—and are recovering."

Something in his gaze then, something more than his
customary consideration, held her very still. Marian
was scarcely aware of the few people near them.

"I wish," she continued impulsively, "I wish you were
not ill. I wish—"

"You mustn't wish for too much, Miss Ware," he said
simply. "I tend to be superstitious."

But he was looking at her so openly that Marian could
only be impatient with the suddenly distracting eruption
of noise from the ballroom. And then Lord Benjamin
stood highlighted against the brilliantly lantern-lit doorway.

"Sidley!" he urged. "Do come. It's Vaughn!"

Chapter Four

"Curses," Sidley muttered again, brushing past Benjamin. Inside all was heat, light, chatter, and company—everything, in fact, that Sidley had gratefully escaped out-of-doors. Miss Ware would have deserted him. . . . Yet as he glanced back over his shoulder, he spotted her several steps behind him. She was holding his cane, which she had thoughtfully retrieved. He paused long enough to allow her to draw even with him, and he gave her the briefest of smiles as she proffered the cane. Though he did not need it for walking, he thought it might serve admirably to brain Vaughn.

"Where is he?" he hissed to Benny, even as their urgency forced the ballroom crowd to give way to them.

Benny nodded toward the hall. "I'd just finished speakin' with Formsby," Benny relayed in a low voice, "when I noticed Knox talking to Vaughn outside the supper room. Both of 'em looked steamed, though in different ways, of course, since Vaughn never *looks* much of anythin'. But then Vaughn made for the hall. I could tell he meant to leave, Sidley, not to cause a scene. Only Knox had to rush after 'im, and I came for you—"

"Well judged, Benny," Sidley murmured just as he entered the hall to confront a red-faced Griffin Knox blocking the door to the Viscount Vaughn.

"I say you shall not leave here without such a promise!" Knox fumed.

"You need no promise, Knox," Vaughn said tightly. "You imagine—"

"Ah! There you are, Vaughn! Good fellow!" Sidley called, forcing an obliviously cheerful smile. "I know we were to depart ten minutes ago—"

"You should never have come at all," Knox snapped. "And now you'd best stay out of this, Sidley."

Sidley's grin lost a bit of its expansiveness. "The last person to *order* me so, Mr. Knox," he said pleasantly, "was a general."

"And what did he say?" Knox sneered. "Polish my boots?"

Sidley leaned heavily on his cane to keep himself from swinging it. "I may misremember," he said easily. "It has been some time, after all. But I believe we were before Orthez, and he wished me to trounce Marshal Soult."

He spoke carelessly, but in that happy company the

comment shocked. And all recognized the battle, just months before, in which Wellington himself had been injured.

In the subsequent silence, Knox's sneer fled. "This is not your affair," he bit out.

"Nor is it Lord Vaughn's."

"It should not be—but he must busy himself where he is not wanted."

Sidley thrust his cane across Vaughn's boots to prevent him from surging toward Knox. Sidley was conscious of the gathering audience and most conscious, perhaps, of Marian Ware several steps beyond his right shoulder. That he should be so alive to her presence was most peculiar.

"This is not the place to air your dispute," Sidley said to Knox. "Lady Katherine and her family can only thank us if we remove ourselves. Will you not step outside an instant, Mr. Knox?"

"I will not leave my wife!"

Sidley's gaze noted Jenny Knox, attended by several friends, at the entrance to the ballroom. "Mrs. Knox is in good company."

"I make certain of it!" Knox spat. "Which is why I'll have that promise from your friend!" He looked at Vaughn, whose lips were tight—as though he meant never to speak again.

Sidley glanced again at Jenny Knox, whose dark eyes were huge in her pale face. Her ghastly pallor gave him an idea.

"Come now, Vaughn," he coaxed in as pompously wheedling a tone as he could manage. He patted Vaughn's sleeve condescendingly. "Surely you can promise the man, fool though he is, anything he likes?"

Vaughn actually frowned. "Leave off, Sidley," he said sharply.

"Good heavens! That from you, when I've—exerted myself so—" Abruptly he loosed his grip on Vaughn's sleeve and, collapsing as heavily as he could against his friend, slid in an apparent faint toward the floor.

Vaughn was quick enough to grab his arms, sparing him a blow to the head. Sidley kept his eyes closed and heard all the hubbub around him: Benny's gleefully repeated "Get back!"; Edgar Formsby's "What has happened?"; and, most clearly, young Lady Katherine's penetrating shriek of "Sidley!", at which he could scarcely prevent himself from cringing.

Sidley heard Vaughn ordering the carriage to be called, then several people were carrying him, unevenly and most uncomfortably, to the door. He heard Colonel Bassett's blistering description of Lord Sidley as a "useless bit of goods," with a dismissive, "Marshal Soult? Most unlikely!" added for good measure.

Even in the darkness out-of-doors he kept his eyes closed, knowing that Edgar Formsby, if not volunteering so much as to help carry him, was enough of a host to see an ill guest from the door. Sidley was doubly glad of his discipline when he heard Marian Ware softly recommending that someone loosen Lord Sidley's collar, and

Vaughn's answering assurance, "We shall see to him, Miss Ware."

Oh, no doubt, no doubt, Sidley thought. The arms that shoved him unceremoniously onto the carriage seat were certainly far from gentle.

"I shall kill you for this," Vaughn muttered darkly as the horses started.

"Why, Vaughn?" Sidley asked, struggling to sit up. "Did you not wish to quit the place?"

Benny laughed, but Vaughn looked like thunder. "You must drop the game with *me,* Lee. I would have left Knox on my own terms, without your interference."

"That is no doubt the case, my friend. But as I stand your second, I deem it my duty to make certain that your 'terms,' as you call them, are not aired. I shall make every effort to prevent a confrontation."

"I would not have challenged Knox."

"Perhaps not. But I fear he comes too close to challenging you. And I have a marginal preference for keeping you whole. In any event," he added, attempting to right his cravat by touch, "the Formsbys' insipid do grew tiresome. It was time to leave."

Benny beamed. "Shall we go on to Boodle's, then, Sidley? You said if we stopped in at Formsby's—"

"Unfortunately, Benny, that plan was previous to my collapse before half the *ton.* Credibility—a precious commodity, my young friend—requires that we retire to Sidley House for the nonce. But by tomorrow I shall have made a miraculous recovery."

"A veritable Lazarus," Vaughn muttered. Even in the limited glow of the carriage lights, Sidley could see how grim he still looked.

"I will call 'round at the Formsbys' tomorrow and make my apologies, Vaughn."

"You should be making your farewells."

Sidley shrugged. "Certainly I can no longer entertain the notion of offering for Lady Katherine. I cannot wed a woman who shrieks so."

"Perhaps *she* mustn't suffer a husband who swoons so."

As Benny laughed again, Vaughn continued to hold Sidley's amused gaze. "It is not Lady Katherine you must bid adieu, as you well know, Lee. You're too much the gentleman to sport with Miss Ware. You are far from insensible. You heard her tonight."

"Yes," Sidley said. "She's very kind—"

" 'Kind'? Don't play with her, Sidley. Let her spend her sympathies on her lieutenant. No doubt they make a charming couple. Be wise enough to take your own advice, else I shall ignore it as well."

"Fair enough, Vaughn." Sidley sighed. "But the girl is invited to Aldersham. What would you have me do about that?"

Vaughn shot him a dark look and shook his head. "Do not go to Aldersham," he suggested.

"We could run on down to Brighton instead!" Benny urged. "Tip Newell and Percy Rutherford went down last week, along with—"

"We are promised to my aunt," Sidley reminded them. "Aldersham it is. I believe I can be dismissive enough to Miss Ware in my own home, with a dozen others about."

"Or private enough," Vaughn suggested.

"I promise you, Vaughn, after tomorrow's call, Miss Ware shall have such an aversion to me, she shan't wish to remain within thirty paces."

The next day they were so dutifully early to pay a call upon the Formsby household that the ladies were not yet available to receive them. Sidley had taken special care with his toilette, being most particular to discard some of his habitual powder, thus improving his outward appearance of health. Intending to abide by his promise to Vaughn, he had also taken care to dress elaborately enough to raise Miss Ware's disapproving eyebrows—though, as he remembered, she had rather nice eyebrows, and he saw no reason to mimic the impudent coxcombs he found so trying.

They were shown into a small front parlor, one obviously rarely used for company, as the ladies' sewing baskets were neatly arrayed to one side of a cold hearth. The gentlemen could hear the preparations for visitors in the drawing room across the hall; undoubtedly the clearing up from the previous night's ball required that callers be diverted temporarily from any lingering evidence of revelry.

"They might at least have lit the fire," Benny grumbled.

"We are rather early, Benny," Sidley told him affably,

"and it is not cold." His gaze had settled on a pair of painted landscapes above the room's fine spinet. He walked over to take a closer look. The neat signature *M. Ware* did not surprise him.

"They are good," Vaughn commented at his side. "She paints like a man."

"She paints better than a man, Vaughn. She paints with the best." Again he concentrated on the perfect water-colors. "These are exquisite."

He heard Vaughn's sigh and turned to him with a quizzical brow. "What is the problem?"

"You, Sidley. You are the problem. Tell me that you have not just abandoned your good intentions." When Sidley stayed silent, Vaughn charged, "You are supposed to be dying. You might act it."

"Vaughn!" He watched Vaughn walk to a corner across the room, where another painting commanded attention. Sidley wished for better light in which to judge the oil, but the beauty of the piece would have been discernible even in the worst surroundings. Depicting the city from across the river, in a scene reminiscent of the prints Sidley had extolled in the *Microcosm,* this rendition was even more beautiful.

"Miss Ware is much too modest," Sidley said.

"She did this?" Benny exclaimed. "How?"

"With a paintbrush and considerable talent. And a perseverance that would be foreign to you, my friend." Sidley turned to face Benny. "Your education has been lacking in certain areas, my lord Benny. We must take a close tour of my collection at home. Or, better yet, visit the summer exhibition at Somerset House."

As Benny protested that he had no time for such frivolities, the butler addressed them from the doorway, with an announcement that the ladies were receiving. They crossed the hall, to be met immediately upon entering the drawing room by a bounding and happily smiling Lady Katherine.

"My lords." She curtsied to them all, then fixed a sparkling gaze on Sidley. "Lord Sidley, I am so pleased to see you recovered."

He waved a hand. "'Twas merely a bit hot in your rooms last night," he claimed, "and I had been exercisin'." His glance slid past a silently attentive Marian Ware, to settle on Lady Formsby. He bowed to the older woman, as did Benny and Vaughn. "Lady Formsby, we must thank you for an excessively fine evening. I apologize for the excitement. I repeat, 'twas nothing."

"Nothing!" Lady Katherine exclaimed. "Why—"

"We are most grateful for your call here today, my lord Sidley," her mother interrupted, with a sharp glance at her boisterous daughter. "'Tis most reassuring. We feared for your health."

"A most misplaced concern, my lady," Sidley told her, but he noticed that the disclaimer did not erase the concern from her face or Miss Ware's. At least Lady Katherine's wide green gaze was untroubled; but then, nothing much ever appeared to trouble the girl.

"I was so glad that you—all of you—could attend last

night," she said. "Mama had given up on you," she added, at which Lady Formsby looked her disapproval. "But I told her you were sure to come, as you'd promised! I do hope you sampled some of our chef's supper. Oh, but you could not have had time! The music was delightful, nonetheless, was it not? I believe Lord Benjamin still owes me that dance," she said, and she paused to grin roguishly at Benny, who went red to his ears.

As additional callers were announced and welcomed, Sidley walked over to Marian Ware, who had retreated to a window alcove. She examined his face with a thoroughness that very nearly undid him.

"You are quite well, then, my lord?" she asked.

"Quite. Or at least—as well as the usual."

"Yes. Yes, I see." She bit her lower lip, which action had the unfortunate effect of drawing his attention.

"Miss Ware," he said abruptly, "we must do something about your painting."

"Do something, my lord?" She smiled. "Do you urge me to improve?"

"You must not languish in parlors."

"You refer to—?"

"Your work, which should be exhibited."

"Those paintings were gifts to my cousins."

"If you have others, they should not be tucked into dark corners."

"I am most flattered, Lord Sidley. But you do me too much honor."

"Nonsense!" He struck his cane forcibly upon the

floor. Immediately he regretted it. He kept his gaze on the rest of the startled company as he spoke tensely, and very low, to Miss Ware. "There are few women who are *painters*. You are one of them. You must permit me to aid you."

"Aid me?" And for a second she looked all of the uncomprehending twenty that she was. "Why, my lord? Because of—because of Lady Katherine?"

Marian watched the impatience creep into Sidley's gaze.

"Lady Katherine! What has she to do with anything?"

Fortunately, this rather rude response was not audible enough to be overheard.

"Really, my lord, I thought that you and she—that if you harbored plans . . ."

"I harbor no plans, Miss Ware. You must put that from your mind. Your painting has naught to do with any of it."

"I would certainly agree, my lord. Though I might ask what, then, other than an interest in my cousin, prompts you to honor the Formsbys with your company."

"I am not accustomed to having my motives or actions so questioned," he said testily.

"I do not mean to do so, my lord. Nevertheless, you must know that my cousin's expectations have been . . . excited."

"If they have been so 'excited,' I am sorry for it," he bit out. "Must we quarrel?"

"I was not aware we quarreled," she countered softly.

Immediately his shoulders eased. He gave her a smile. "Certainly not," he agreed. Again he surveyed the drawing room, where additional callers were filling out the company. "Still, I must be permitted to further your interests. Perhaps—well, I might ease an introduction. If you could paint anyone of your acquaintance here in town, Miss Ware, whom would you choose?"

Marian looked up at his profile, only to meet his penetrating gaze as he turned to her once more. "You expect me to say I would paint *you*, Lord Sidley."

"On the contrary. You *will* paint me. I have decided that there is no choice involved in it. My query was intended to understand your eye, to elicit your preferences in subject."

Marian had to look away from him, lest he perceive that she might easily *choose* to paint him, which, of course, she had no intention of doing. "You have no notion of my ability with a likeness."

"On the contrary," he claimed. "I have more than a notion. I have come to a belief."

She swallowed. No one, not even her father, had ever expressed so much faith in her.

"Then I might—I think perhaps I might wish to paint Mrs. Knox," she admitted.

"Ah!" Sidley's smile was resigned rather than pleased. His gaze sought Viscount Vaughn. "In that you are not unusual. Mrs. Knox is a rare beauty. But you shall have some difficulty portraying her as she ought to be portrayed." He paused. "There were several portraits made of Jenny Lanning even before she became Mrs. Knox. And her husband has subsequently employed every painter of fashion—which is his style."

There was a bite to his tone. Marian wished she understood the reason for the previous night's altercation. Her aunt had not known, and now Lord Sidley seemed disinclined to enlighten her. She could not believe he nursed a *tendre* for the woman, acknowledged diamond though she was. But something was very wrong.

Abruptly he asked, "You will be at Aldersham next week?"

"As you know, my lord, I have only a brief time in which to study. I regret that I must decline the invitation."

"You might paint at Aldersham almost as well as you do in town. Perhaps better." He smiled. "The light is infinitely clearer."

"Even if that's the case, I fear I must explain to your aunt that I cannot attend."

"My aunt does not listen to explanations, Miss Ware," which attribute Marian thought might equally apply to Lady Adeline's nephew. But he smiled as Katie approached them. "Lady Katherine," he said with a nod.

"You must not keep Lord Sidley from the rest of the company, Marian!" Katie admonished. Her brief glance at Marian was annoyed. "You had his time yesterday evening."

"So I did, Katie. My lord." And Marian excused herself. She sought refuge at the other end of the room, but her attention inevitably returned to Katie and Lord Sidley by the window. She noted Katie's irrepressible efforts and Sidley's forced smile. Marian knew that Katie would see only the smile, not the impatience behind it, and silently counseled her cousin to let the man be. But Katie would believe Sidley just another enchanted admirer.

He has grown tired of this, Marian thought in sudden sympathy, only to have his gaze flash to her own. She fought her blush and concentrated on the conversation at hand. Yes, she agreed, the summer promised to be unusually warm. Yes, the celebrations of Bonaparte's abdication were very grand. Yes, Lady Katherine's ball had been the best attended of the season. Indeed, Katie was destined to make a brilliant match. But what did Miss Ware think—did not Lady Katherine look well paired with Lord Sidley?

Marian could only smile. An attachment was Katie's stated goal, one that Lord Sidley seemed sadly reluctant to share.

Viscount Vaughn spoke with her briefly about Northampton, asking after any news she had had from the Navy. Marian wondered if Vaughn deliberately introduced the topic, as a means of reminding her of William. But Lord Vaughn was all politeness; there was no reason to suspect he believed she required a reminder. Her own sense of disloyalty should have been reminder enough. Lord Benjamin joined them, with an enthusiastic compliment of the lemon comfit cakes and an unanswerable question as to how much "perseverance" one needed in order to paint.

Lady Formsby's west drawing room never grew too crowded, for it had been designed for entertaining and was suitably large. Nevertheless, courtesy required that even in the aftermath of so stellar an event as Katherine's ball, visitors should confine their calls to a scarce twenty minutes or less. After the requisite period, Marian noticed Lord Sidley moving toward the doors and his escape, though Katie had been so bold as to attempt to stay him with a hand on his velvet sleeve. Through whatever subtle cues the three gentlemen communicated, Lord Benjamin and Lord Vaughn seemed aware of Sidley's determination to depart. Within moments they had made their bows to Lady Formsby, and Katie, though a dozen more attentive suitors filled the room, was left to pout.

As Marian approached her, Katie was saying: "As he's offering, he ought to act a bit more—a bit more—"

"Hush, child," her mother warned. "Do not speak so here in company. Whatever are you thinking?"

Katie tossed her bright curls as she gazed disconsolately upon the remaining callers. "Perhaps I should make him jealous," she said, boldly eyeing two young gentlemen standing in a window embrasure.

"You have not learned such tricks from me, Katherine," her mother said sharply, "nor from anyone of sense."

Katie turned to Marian. "Did Lord Sidley speak of me, Marian?"

"He said he looked forward to our company at Aldersham," she relayed truthfully. "He was most insistent on it."

As Katie smiled, her mother said, "Before you congratulate yourself too heartily, my dear, remember that his aunt has invited some other eligible young ladies."

Katie's chin rose as she prepared to dismiss any threat, but a footman clearing beverage glasses interrupted.

"Pardon, mum, but I believe Lord Sidley just left his walking stick." He raised Sidley's cane. "Shall I—"

Marian promptly grabbed the cane. "I shall take it out to Jenks at the door, Aunt," she said, as she moved quickly toward the hall. "We might yet catch him." In truth, she wished to escape Katie's gloating and considered the errand a respite.

But Jenks was not at the door. He and two footmen were down at the curb, assisting a vocal Lady Addlestrop from her fashionable landau. Marian's anxious gaze caught Sidley with his companions farther along the pavement—walking, she noted, rather well without the aid of his prop. Swiftly she stepped down to the street. Handing the cane to the tallest Formsby footman, she instructed him to hail Lord Sidley immediately and race to return it to him.

The footman dutifully shouted and set off, but in the crowd promenading on the sidewalk, Marian could not see whether Sidley had stopped. Lady Addlestrop's descent was creating a noisy disturbance behind her, and there were several excited cries that the visiting tsar's entourage was passing. Marian moved to the very edge of the street to watch for Sidley. She knew she ought to return to the drawing room, her task had been fulfilled, but the afternoon air was fresh and balmy and infinitely more appealing than more of Katie's preening.

Again she heard the footman shout, "M'lord Sidley!"

Then Sidley appeared at the curb, looking back toward Marian's position. She waved but feared he had not seen her in the crowd. So she stepped into the street, which was blessedly dry and free of mud. The reward for exposing herself so was a smile from Sidley, who raised the restored cane in salute.

But as the Addlestrop commotion increased in volume, as cheers arose for some passing dignitary in the square, Sidley's smile vanished. He, too, stepped into the street, calling out an alarmed "Marian!" even as she turned to face the roadway.

The landau's team was acting up, the near horse was rearing in its traces, while the coachman attempted to haul the animal back. But the heavy carriage was still drifting unbidden to the center of the street, where two wildly racing curricles vied for precedence in the narrow, packed turning off the square.

The din from pounding hooves, the chattering crowd, and anxious, whinnying animals was deafening. Before Marian could reach the safety of the sidewalk, she was tossed there in a pained, ungainly heap. Appalled screams heralded the collapse of a heavy male form beside her. As she pushed herself from the pavement on shaking hands, Marian stared in dazed disbelief at the bloody rent in Sidley's buckskins, just above one knee. His face lay still and pale against the stone. Whether she managed to speak then she could not have said, but her mind repeated numbly, *I have killed him, I have killed him, I have killed him. . . .*

Chapter Five

"A regular Hercules!" Edgar enthused. "That's what they're callin' 'im. Tossin' you about like that while snaffling old Addlestrop's nag! Horse should be turned over to the knacker after acting up that way. Might've killed him, and you too, though I 'spose Mopes and Carroll shouldn't a' been racing just then, and there—"

"I should say not!" Edith agreed. "Do stop this, Edgar. We know how impressed you are with Lord Sidley's prowess. We are most grateful for it. Indeed, I can never thank him enough. But you must see that the reminder upsets Marian."

"Your pardon, cousin." Edgar nodded to Marian in the carriage seat opposite. "I thought you'd want to know, though, as you—as you couldn't *see* it."

Marian, who still felt the bruises from her rescue the

week before, smiled wanly. In truth, she had not *seen* much of anything, though she had heard and felt enough to keep her occupied for some time.

She had feared for Sidley. But he had lived, and so had she, and because he had placed her under so very great an obligation, she was now compelled to accompany her family to Aldersham. In any other circumstance she'd have successfully regretted the invitation and avoided the place, or so she had convinced herself.

"I don't see why Marian had to make such a scene," Katie observed. "And not for the first time. 'Twas ridiculous for her to be hopping about in the street at all!"

"Yes, Katie. I was foolish beyond measure. Which only increases my debt to Lord Sidley. A more rational man would have left me to my fate."

"I will never forget how quickly he moved," Edgar said, shifting once more into worshipful tones. "A fellow forgets he's at death's door. Though one can only suppose that now he's even more—What? Oh. Sorry." And as his mother glared at him, Edgar lapsed into silence.

They had almost reached Aldersham, their journey into Kent having taken the better part of two days at the dawdling pace Lady Formsby deemed decorous. Now Marian felt Edith's gaze upon her averted profile.

"You will enjoy yourself, Marian," she said, more in the nature of a command than of encouragement.

Marian attempted a smile as she turned from viewing the county's rolling hills and gracefully shaded lanes.

"I'm sure I shall, Aunt. Whether I am as successful at continuing my painting is another matter."

"You have your whole life in which to paint, my dear. I suspect that future invitations to Sidley's Aldersham are much less likely."

"Oh, but, Mama, I shall be inviting Marian and all my friends at every opportunity!" Katie said.

Edgar snorted dismissively. "A false start, there, Missy Kate," he said with a superior look at his sister. "The betting book at White's has better odds on two other chits. And I can't say as I'd blame Sidley for choosin' either of them instead."

"I know better, *Mr. Peacock*," Katie scoffed. "During this stay at his aunt's I shall convince him that I would make the finest countess."

"Then he'd be the only one convinced of it!"

"Edgar . . ." his mother warned. "I do hope you two will make some effort at civility. Marian and I are unfortunately too accustomed to these squabbles; we've learned to ignore them. But should you be overheard at Aldersham, your wishes and wagers and other plans are like to come to naught. Mind me—both of you simply must be more guarded."

Both her cousins settled back, looking chastened. Marian felt chastened as well, but for another reason. Just before their departure from town, she had at last received a letter from William; he had told her he expected to return by the end of the fortnight. His letter had in all ways been very much like every letter he had ever sent her, yet Marian had wanted more—some greater degree of warmth, perhaps, or of anticipation. After such a lengthy absence, they were at last to begin their life together. To her increasingly critical sensibility that merited a more personal closing than: *Most eager to see you. As ever, Wm.*

As ever. As ever. The carriage wheels mocked the refrain. She should not have expected an eagerness on William's part that she was far from feeling herself. For this past year she had contentedly considered her prospects settled; she had been free to pursue her craft. But in light of her unlooked-for reactions to Lord Sidley, that view of marriage now seemed less practical than narrowly acquisitive. Yes, it was best she relieve her brother and his future wife of the responsibility for a spinster sister. But marrying in friendship, to secure a position, no longer appealed. And though William might now find sufficient satisfaction in the arrangement, he might not always.

Neither of them had ever spoken of love. Yet love . . . For some reason love consumed Marian's thoughts.

Along the roadway the afternoon sunlight bathed Kent's fields and ancient hedgerows in warmth. Marian felt she *must* succeed in painting at Aldersham, if only to remove herself as frequently as possible from the weekend party. For Katie had relayed every word of gossip concerning the other aspirants for Lord Sidley's favor. And Katie, Marian reflected in some surprise, had shown a remarkable dedication to accumulating news about her reported rivals. Indeed, competition had focused most powerfully her frivolous cousin's attentions. Two names in particular had surfaced in serious contention. Just how Katie intended to use her research was another matter, and one with which Marian was not at all certain she wished to be familiar.

"Forewarned is forearmed," Katie had claimed, glibly quoting the Cervantes that she had never troubled to read. But whereas Lady Katherine, daughter of an earl, might well feel she had quite an arsenal at her command, Miss Marian Ware of Brinford did not.

She had to stop herself from laughing at the thought of her palette and brushes as weapons, only to remind herself that she was not truly one of the party. Lord Sidley would not grant Marian Ware the same consideration he gave Miss Delia Tinckney-Dwight.

Katie had singled out the young woman at a soiree just days before. Delia's father, Sir Philip Tinckney-Dwight, having served the king in some inestimable manner, had garnered both position and fortune. But Delia's brilliant season several years before had been unhappily cut short by her mother's illness. Now, as a recent widower, Sir Philip was rumored to be applying himself, with the same fervor that had brought him a knighthood, to achieving a consequential match for his daughter. From all she had heard and the little she had seen, Marian considered Delia to be Katie's most formidable rival.

The other name circulating in the betting books was Rebecca Harvey's. Though reputedly not as lovely as

Lady Katherine, eighteen-year-old Becca had endeared herself to the gentlemen with a reputation as a neck-or-nothing rider. Her considerable fortune of 100,000 pounds also did not go unremarked. True, her parents, having gained their wealth in trade, still lacked a prestigious country property. And Marian's cousin Edith, who was usually most forgiving, had declared Mrs. Harvey to be an irritating, ingratiating "mushroom." But the Harveys' wealth would be all too welcome to many impoverished peers. Marian did not know the state of the Sidley finances—proper young ladies did not know such things—but she had to imagine that a well-placed 100,000 pounds would never be scorned. She recalled Colonel Bassett's comment at the Hempthorne card party, that Sidley lacked "wherewithal," and the colonel's reference to the appalling state of Sidley House in town. Though Colonel Bassett's information had proved unreliable in other respects, Marian had to conclude that Lord Sidley did indeed need funds, else this haste to wed in his waning days made little sense.

Again she reminded herself that she did not care, that the matter did not concern her. She determined to spend as little time as possible in company with the misses Harvey and Tinckney-Dwight.

"Marian!" Katie nudged her. "You are woolgathering again! I have asked you twice if you remembered to bring your silhouette shears." The small, delicate pair served admirably for rendering the popular cut-paper profiles.

"I did. But Katie, 'tis not a pastime this sophisticated group is likely to find entertaining."

"Such stuff! You could not be more wrong. Everyone wishes to have at least one likeness." Katie happened to have several. "And yours are always much commended." As Katie invariably volunteered Marian's talents, Marian was resigned to the performances; at least they gave her practice, though the entertainment did sometimes border on drudgery. "I believe we shall all have a very merry time of it," Katie added.

"I do not understand how you can be so cheerful," Marian said. "There is something—something gruesome about this situation. As though everyone were chasing after a casket."

"That is too bleak of you, Marian," Edith said. "Lady Adeline would never have countenanced visitors at Aldersham if Lord Sidley were wasting so very—so very rapidly. And to have saved you as he did—well, perhaps we have been misinformed."

"No doubt he is that much closer to expiring after the exertion," Marian observed glumly.

"But I had it that he was never even ill abed," Edgar said, "and came on here days ago. He must have a few more weeks in 'im. . . ." He fell silent as they pulled into a curved gravel drive.

Aldersham was a revelation. Marian had anticipated a ruin, a building that would in some manner reflect the various tragedies that had befallen the Sidley family. But the house itself, an expansive, three-story Elizabethan stone with tall mullioned windows, impressive gabled wings and attic dormers, was magnificent and welcoming at once. In the afternoon light the ancient stone glowed with gold highlights. Scaffolding enclosed one farther wing, though workmen were absent at the moment, and the grounds were clearly under reconstruction. But the estate had not been abandoned, as Marian had supposed. All the glorious windows sparkled, and to one side of the house a well-tended rose garden, perhaps Lady Adeline's pet, exhibited attentive, continuous care.

"You see, children?" Edith breathed as the carriage stopped in front of the entrance. "Aldersham is still something to admire."

Standing before the house in the drive, Marian gazed up at the old gray stone, which, viewed at close quarters, supported subtly-colored lichen. She wheeled to view the enclosing lawns, woods, and prospects. Her eagerness to explore made her giddy.

Inside, the house did not disappoint. Being some centuries old, it had inevitable oddities in the size and shape of rooms, the evenness of plaster, and the spacing of steps and lintels. But all lent charm, and the many leaded windows permitted an astonishing amount of light, which Marian would never have anticipated in such an old place.

"Must have cost them a fortune," Edgar muttered, tilting his head to survey the two-story high glass in a banqueting room off the hall. "No wonder Sidley's look-ing for an heiress," he added, which comment suffi-ciently doused Marian's enthusiasm.

She and Katie were shown to their bedrooms and large sitting room above, with a northerly view of a gently sloped valley and nestled village. Katie was at first dis-posed to object to the room, until Marian pointed out that it would be cooler during the increasingly warm June days. And the light—the light was clear and generous through a doubled front of windows. When Marian no-ticed that a dressing table sat at a somewhat awkward an-gle away from the windows, she wondered if Lord Sidley had requested the space cleared, in the event that she might wish to work in the room. She was convinced of it when the manservant brought in their trunks and, without any direction from them, placed Marian's paint box be-neath the windows.

It was almost six. They were told that dinner would be served in an hour. As they oversaw some unpacking and changed out of their travel clothes, Marian was grateful, as she had never been before, for Edith's insistence on gifting her with a wardrobe, even for the short stay in town. Without her new belongings, she would have felt much at a disadvantage. As it was, she knew the other guests' garments would easily eclipse even her precious lutestring gown, which she had donned only once before—three weeks ago for the Osbornes' rout. Again she pointedly reminded herself that she did not signify.

"You look beautiful, Katie," she said as the maid finished dressing her cousin's glorious hair.

"I do hope to make an impression," Katie confided, turning from a seat at the dressing table to face her. "In a smaller group such as this, he must see me at my best."

"It is a very select group," Marian cautioned.

"I am convinced it is solely for appearances, to satisfy his old aunt. I have every expectation, Marian." With a sigh of contentment, Katie eyed her critically. "You look very well, though I do wonder that Mama had you select such a gown. You will have few opportunities to wear it."

"I am wearing it now," Marian countered, though the comment was—unintentionally, she knew—hurtful. She forced a smile. "And perhaps I shall wear it soon again— at your wedding."

Katie smiled back at her reflection in the glass. "I am delighted with Aldersham! So fine a site. And the improvements should not take long."

"The improvements?"

"Only those most necessary, of course. But you must agree, the place is fusty beyond bearing. So many smallish rooms! I must look closely when we go down, but I know I shall wish to add decorative work to the walls, and more drapes about all the windows. One feels like a fish in a bowl! And all the dreary stone shall have to be covered by stucco, of course. You've such excellent taste, Marian, I know I will be wanting your help."

No, Marian objected silently. *By the time you are*

destroying Aldersham, I shall hope to be at least a hundred miles away.

When they went down to join the company, Marian was at first concerned that the group looked too large; she wished only to retreat for the entirety of the stay. But as she and Katie made their way into the drawing room, she realized that she belonged to the extensive Formsby party, which, with four, was larger than any.

Lord Sidley was absent, which prompted Marian to recognize how much she had wished to see him again, and to see him in health. But his friends Lord Vaughn and Lord Benjamin were in attendance and being most solicitous with Edith and another older lady who could only be Sidley's aunt. Marian thought Lady Adeline's features striking, feminine yet strong. Though her hair was graying, it had obviously once been as dark as her nephew's.

Aunt Edith beckoned them over. "Adeline, you know my daughter, Katherine." Katie bobbed. "But you have not met my young cousin, Marian Ware."

"Miss Ware." Lady Adeline acknowledged Marian's curtsey. "Edith tells me she was most fond of your mother. A Satterthwaite, I believe?"

"Yes, ma'am. And a Ware."

"I understand you favor her."

"I've been told so, my lady."

"You must forgive Sidley, Miss Ware. I believe he intended to present you to me, but as you see, he is not yet down."

"No doubt he had no wish to disappoint his guests,

ma'am," Marian said, and Lady Adeline's eyebrows rose expectantly, "by dressing in too much haste."

Lady Adeline smiled. "I suspect you have the right of it, Miss Ware." She looked her up and down. "You are an artist."

"Yes."

Again Lady Adeline smiled. "I hope you shall find Aldersham to your liking."

"Aldersham is splendid, my lady. And inspiring. I hope to paint the grounds."

"Sidley speaks of having you draw his portrait."

"He claims so, yes, my lady."

"If he claims so, Miss Ware, you may depend upon its eventual accomplishment. You do not mind?"

"I am honored."

"I imagine he is the one so honored," she said kindly. "Would you be troubled were I to observe you?"

"Not at all—if it does not distract Lord Sidley."

"The day I manage to distract Sidley, my dear, I shall consider myself to have succeeded in life." As she laughed, Marian smiled in surprise. She had not anticipated that Lady Adeline Pell would be so frank. "Now I must let you be introduced to the rest of our guests, Miss Ware, but I look forward to speaking with you further."

Marian moved on with Katie and Edgar to greet Rebecca Harvey and her rather too obviously pleased parents. Lord Benjamin, hovering nearby, paid enough homage to the girl to present some nature of challenge to a smitten Edgar. Though Becca seemed unmoved by either gentleman's flattery, Marian and Katie still exchanged glances.

"This will not be to Mama's liking," Katie whispered as they moved on to the next group of guests. "You've heard her comments on Mrs. Harvey. . . ."

"I am certain it is just a temporary flirt, Katie. Edgar has been impressed with several young ladies even during the few weeks I've been in town."

"Oh, but the Harveys!"

"Please, Katie. Not here."

By the windows looking out to the rose garden, Sir Philip Tinckney-Dwight stood with his daughter, Delia, and a young couple, the Pooles, unknown to Marian and Katie. They learned that the Pooles, brother and sister, whose parents had been off in India many years, lived not far from Aldersham. As Katie conversed with them, Marian was once again struck by Delia's perfection. Though clearly not as pretty as Katie, Delia had a calm, courteous manner that was elegant. Indeed, the word *countess* came instantly to mind, as though the word were stamped across her features and her future. And Sir Philip, a distinguished man of height and lean good looks, acted as though Aldersham were already a second home.

"Miss Ware," he said pleasantly, "I have heard much of you from my friend Lord Lascelles, who supports the Royal Academy."

"That is most kind of him, sir. I thank you."

"Had Delia shown an ounce of talent in that direction, I'd have been delighted."

"I am certain Miss Tinckney-Dwight has many other talents," Marian said.

And Delia acknowledged the compliment with a smile.

"I play the harp," Katie offered rather too eagerly. "Do you play an instrument, Miss Tinckney-Dwight?"

"The pianoforte, Lady Katherine. But I do not play nearly as well as Miss Poole here, who is a proficient. I much prefer vocals."

"Perhaps we might have some music one evening from the ladies," Richard "Dicky" Poole said to Sir Philip. "In fact, the convenience of a trio suggests Sidley planned it."

"Here, we might ask him," Sir Philip said.

And Marian turned with the rest of them to note Lord Sidley's entrance.

She had anticipated that he would again dress to the nines, as she had last seen him on the day after Katie's ball. But he surprised her. This evening his garb was quieter but no less refined, a superbly tailored black coat and trousers and a pewter-colored waistcoat. His complexion was almost as pale as his cravat, but his smile, and the diamond pin at his throat, sparkled.

Marian was fascinated to watch how quickly the three separate groups in the drawing room gathered as one about Lord Sidley. The attraction was not merely that of a host, for she recalled the sensation he had caused at the bookstore and at Katie's ball. She watched his eager guests and wondered how she should paint such effortless appeal; she wondered if it would reveal itself on a flat canvas—if she were even capable of capturing so immaterial an attribute. Close on that thought came another that was wildly reassuring; others reacted to Lord Sidley just as she did—she was not the only one susceptible. So when he briefly caught her gaze and smiled, she did not crumple to the floor.

He tapped his cane against that floor and addressed Lady Adeline. "My dear aunt, why have we no carpet?"

"You'll recall we ordered a new one, Sidley, due within the week. You thought it more fitting for a blue room."

"Ah, yes. Well, my friends, what do you think of watered silk upon old Aldersham's walls?" He waved at the drawing room walls. All agreed that the subtle color, obviously just applied, was most appropriate.

"But, Lord Sidley, as the floor is bare, perhaps we might have dancing in here?" Katie boldly voiced the request.

"Indeed, Lady Katherine, a charming idea. Though I believe our numbers—ladies over gentlemen, that is—are somewhat uneven, particularly as my steps have proved the same."

Again Marian felt his quick glance, but she looked away.

"We were just discussing, Sidley," Richard Poole said, "that some of the ladies might provide us with music. M'sister might play the pianoforte."

"Admirable, Dicky. But then who should play the piano when I wish to dance with Miss Clara?"

"I might do that for you, my lord," Delia offered.

Sidley smiled at her. "I do not plan to trouble any of my guests with furnishing entertainment, but the offer is most kind, Miss Delia."

And Marian, hearing his tone and gauging his smile, thought Katie must resign herself to failure.

Katie, however, clearly had no thought of surrender. She insisted on remaining at Sidley's side, even as he moved to greet each of his guests individually, and she seemed to believe her greatest rival was Rebecca Harvey. This despite evidence that Becca was no more partial to Lord Sidley than she had been to Edgar or Lord Benjamin.

"I fear Katie has not read this correctly," Edith whispered softly to Marian. "Do see what you can do to prevent—" She stopped and sighed. "My dear Marian, I suspect there is not much any of us might do."

"It is the first evening, Aunt. Katie will settle. You shall see."

"Ah, but Marian, these first impressions are everything!" She went to speak with the Harveys, which cost her an effort, but an effort that Marian was proud to see was not at all apparent.

Clara and Richard Poole drifted to her spot by the hall door. "What do you think of Aldersham, then, Miss Ware?" Dicky asked.

"It is most impressive. I had heard some talk in town that the estate had fallen to ruin. So you can imagine my astonishment."

"'Tis true the estate has weathered some hard times,"

Dicky said. "But even before his return, Sidley arranged for improvements. His aunt used to spend half of each year here and plans to do so again."

"You know it well, then, Mr. Poole?"

"We live but five miles away, Miss Ware. And I was at school with Sidley's older brother, Simon. Clara and I visited often, before the many tragedies that have beset this family."

Noticing how troubled Clara Poole looked, Marian attempted to engage her by asking if she had been in town during the spring. "Not at all. I was . . . I was indisposed much of this past season," she said softly.

"M'sister was most attached to Simon Pell, Miss Ware," Dicky Poole explained. "His loss was very difficult for everyone. Lee—that is, Lord Sidley—idolized his brother. It has made his situation that much more painful, as you can imagine."

Marian expressed her sympathies. To keep all of them from dwelling on Sidley's painful situation, she asked the Pooles about their home and the country surrounding Aldersham.

"What can you be saying, Miss Ware," Sidley asked on coming up to them, "that has the Pooles looking so solemn? And on our very first night as well! I expected you to thrill them with the latest *on dit*s from town."

"Oh, but *I* might do that!" Katie volunteered.

"If you would be so kind, then, Lady Katherine, as

to cheer the Pooles," Sidley said, "I must reprimand Miss Ware."

Katie laughed and launched upon a tale, while Marian, in some irritation, allowed herself to be led apart. She tried not to think of Sidley's gloved hand upon her bare elbow and, once he released her, concentrated upon his diamond cravat pin.

"At this moment, and for just a moment, none of my guests needs anything at all," he observed easily. And looking over the room, Marian saw that that was indeed the case; none of his guests looked in the least neglected. "Will you not look happy about it?" he asked.

"I must be 'happy' to be reprimanded, my lord?"

"No other lady here has been so distinguished," he said with a smile.

"I should rather not be so 'distinguished,' when I am undeserving."

"Are you undeserving?"

"Of a reprimand, certainly."

"Perhaps. And yet, Miss Ware, I feel I must reprimand you. For yours is a most becoming gown, which you have worn in my presence only once before."

"You are mistaken, my lord. This is the first time I have worn this gown in your presence."

"Is it?"

"It is. The gown was new three weeks ago, Lord Sidley, and I have worn it on only one other occasion—to the Osbornes' rout."

"Yes! Ozzie's rout."

"You did not attend the Osbornes' rout."

"Did I not?"

As she met his gaze, Marian read the amusement there, as well as the truth. He must indeed have attended the Osbornes' rout and remembered her in the gown.

She wondered how she had missed him or, more particularly, how *Katie* had missed him. The Osbornes' had been a noisy, stifling crush, it was true, but failing to note Lord Sidley seemed incomprehensible.

As she gazed up at him, she thought she must look stricken. For she realized might have met him more than a week earlier than she had; she would have delighted in simply knowing *of* him those few additional, precious days.

His own look had sobered. "That will teach you," he said softly, "to ignore the attentions of gentlemen." He glanced away from her. "I see that my aunt gives me the gimlet eye. We must parade ourselves to dinner." And smoothly surrendering Marian to Dicky Poole, who would escort her into the dining room, Sidley freed himself to lend an arm each to both his aunt and hers.

Chapter Six

Vaughn, Sidley thought, could not fault him this evening. He had paid scant attention to the girl, even declining to introduce her to his aunt. And he had given Lady Adeline free rein with the seating, which—following precedent as closely as an informal gathering might allow—placed Miss Ware at the center of the table, practically out of hearing. That Sidley should chafe at the fact was something Vaughn need not know.

Each time she turned to Dicky Poole, on her right, she turned toward Sidley's end of the table. Thus he caught all of her smiles for sunny Richard. There appeared to be too many smiles. And Dicky's manner this evening was much too raffish, out of keeping for the steady country squire he had become.

"Lord Sidley," Mrs. Harvey simpered, drawing his

attention, "you have a most hospitable dining chamber here."

"I thank you, ma'am. I am surprised, as we rarely dine in it. 'Tis rather cavernous for two."

"No doubt that will change, my lord, when you entertain more," Lady Katherine suggested.

"If I do, dear lady, I hope you will often be in the company."

At that she worried her lower lip. Lady Katherine was a lively enough girl, and certainly decorative. Sidley could only hope she would outgrow her affectations— but not, please heaven, on his watch.

He thought he should be particularly attentive to Delia Tinckney-Dwight on his left, as he considered it probable he would be offering for her. But he knew he would not be doing so until Miss Ware had run off with her sailor.

"Goodness, my lord, what a frown!" Katie exclaimed. "Is the idea really so distasteful? I understood from your aunt that you were used to attending the local fair!"

For a moment he could only stare at her. "The fair. Yes. I beg your pardon, Lady Katherine. I have been inattentive. Whatever you might wish will always be acceptable to me. 'Tis a pleasant enough outing. Should you like to try it?"

"Above all things! Perhaps tomorrow, if the weather is fine?"

He gave Lady Katherine a tight smile and turned to Delia. "I know you are well-acquainted with the county, Miss Delia. Have you a fondness for fairs?"

"Indeed, my lord," she said with a smile. Yet what Sidley heard was Marian's voice, farther along that side, teasing—yes, *teasing*—Dicky Poole about the planting of hops. Vaughn, seated to Miss Ware's left, was not distracting her at all, as he was fully occupied in keeping Benny and Lord Formsby from coming to blows over Becca Harvey's attentions.

Though Sidley willed Vaughn to look his way and take direction, the thought alone effected nothing.

"My father's family also is Kentish," Delia was saying with a nod toward her father, involved in a discussion with Clara Poole, who, like Miss Ware, claimed the table's center. "But his people live closer to the channel, near Dover. In fact, on one visit some years ago, we passed by Aldersham en route, and though Lady Adeline was away, took a tour."

"Did you? You must have met our housekeeper, Mrs. Combes."

She nodded. "We were treated most kindly, my lord."

"And how did the place show?"

"To great advantage, I assure you, Lord Sidley, though it was autumn and your magnificent roses were not in bloom. I recall wishing I might return to see them in the proper season."

Sidley wondered whether he should suspect the girl of tailoring her prospects as carefully as Lady Katherine did her own. But he decided that Miss Delia's gaze lacked guile. She had no thought other than to further the conversation in as pleasant a manner as possible.

As he again heard Dicky Poole's laughter, he gave Miss Delia a broad smile. "My aunt is exceedingly fond of her roses. She will give you slips of any you desire."

"I am no gardener, my lord."

"Oh, but I am," Mrs. Harvey asserted. "Do you think Lady Adeline would be so kind as to favor me so, my lord?"

"Lady Adeline is invariably hospitable, ma'am. 'Twould be her pleasure, I'm sure." His aunt had always proved gracious, even when confronted by irritatingly forward guests. For the remainder of the meal he engaged the three ladies in a general conversation on the trimming of bonnets, the proper constitution of ices, and the merits of Scott's various novels. He forced attention to the chatter and limited his glimpses of Miss Ware. Yet he was still relieved when Vaughn claimed both her attention and Clara Poole's.

As Sidley at last caught his aunt's gaze, he signaled a preference for ending dinner, and the ladies abandoned the gentlemen in removing to the drawing room.

His aunt captured him for a few seconds before her own departure. "Do stop scowling, Sidley," she said very low.

"I am not scowling."

"You certainly appear to be so."

"That I cannot help," he claimed. But she was already out of hearing.

Vaughn settled in on his left. "You must rally, Sidley," he said as the gentlemen sipped their port. "You are looking as lovesick as any fresh-cheeked pup, and green with jealousy too."

"I am supposed to be sickening for something, Vaughn. I might as soon look it."

"Poor Dicky Poole does not deserve such glowers."

"Poor Dicky Poole," Sidley countered, "does not appear in the least tormented."

"I know you are newly afflicted, but I shouldn't have expected you to act as juvenile as Benny and Lord Formsby. You might need as strict a hand."

"I'd have welcomed your intervention—had it led you to turn to her more frequently."

Vaughn shook his head. "You've forgotten, my friend, that your impediment is not Dicky but Lieutenant Reeves."

"You must tell me then, Vaughn, how you manage such complexities."

At which Vaughn glared at him and removed himself to the other side of the room.

The reminder, however, did compel Sidley to rise to his duties as a host, to discuss affably the latest mill at Fives Court and the peace terms out of Paris. By the time the gentlemen rejoined the ladies, Sidley had recovered his humor. But he was irritated anew to find Marian Ware engaged in cutting silhouettes for the others, while her cousin hovered near, like any hawker with a popular commodity.

"Is Marian not excellent at catching these profiles, my lord?" Lady Katherine asked.

"She is indeed. But, Miss Ware"—and the girl paused long enough in "catching" Mrs. Harvey to look up at him—"do leave off. We cannot have you taxing yourself so on your very first evening."

"I do not mind it, my lord."

" 'Tis not sufficient that you should not 'mind.' Whatever you do here should elicit greater enthusiasm than *that*. Do abandon this. As you have so eagerly volunteered to start my portrait, I must take you to see the gallery."

"But I haven't—"

He deftly removed the small shears from her hand, then took her elbow and drew her to her feet. "You see how easily 'tis done," he said softly. "You are above such parlor tricks." Her gaze held his, surprise and a desire to dispute with him warring in the changeable dark depths of her eyes.

"I should very much prefer to see the gallery anyway, Lord Sidley," Mrs. Harvey claimed, rising as well.

Sidley felt the insult to Miss Ware; he was tempted to tell the woman that anything bespoke from Miss Ware's hand must always claim preference. But he refrained and turned to his guests, and soon the chattering entourage was making its way along the gallery commemorating all the former earls of Sidley and their relations.

Sidley wished to know what Miss Ware thought of each of the paintings, whether drawn by Van Dyck, Kneller, Gainsborough, Reynolds, Ramsay, or many others. He had grown familiar with them as a boy and had his own particular favorites for style and expression. But she eluded him as he led first Lady Katherine, then Miss Delia, then Clara Poole past the portraits. Miss Becca Harvey he left to Benny and Lord Formsby.

"I think, Lee," Clara said in some amusement, glancing behind them at the Harvey heiress, "that you face an easier choice than your aunt might have imagined."

He followed her gaze to Miss Rebecca. "Never an option, Clara. She is far too young."

"But Lady Katherine is not."

"Lady Katherine is also too young."

Clara's eyebrows rose. "You have decided, then?"

He looked away from her. "I near a conclusion, Clara. But it is hardly a decision. More a necessity."

"That is a shame, Lee. You deserve better."

"As do you." He smiled as he lightly squeezed her arm. "Now tell me, what do you think of Great-grandfather Exbridge?"

"He looks a tartar, as we've always known him to have been! I remember Simon as a boy making faces at him."

As her eyes glistened, Sidley slid an arm about her shoulders. "Simon would have wanted you happy, Clara."

"And you as well, Lee."

"Perhaps the two of us, then . . . Perhaps . . ." But she was firmly shaking her head. And he knew that the suggestion was one he should air only the once. They were friends; they shared grief. But that was not enough. Clara Poole would only ever be a sister.

"Dicky seems most taken with Miss Ware," she commented. "'Twas not what I thought at first, but he is laughing a great deal."

Sidley no longer heard her. The observation disturbed him. That Clara should notice what he thought apparent only to himself annoyed him beyond measure. He thought the attachment troubling enough that, when the party broke up later that evening, he was unduly abrupt as he informed Marian Ware that he would appreciate her appearance, with her paints, in his library the following morning.

Sidley had not stipulated the hour. Marian fretted over that as she collected her painting supplies from the sitting room she and Katie shared. When she stepped quietly downstairs, she suspected she was much too early; she was an early riser in any event. Katie, by contrast, was likely to sleep past noon. But if Lord Sidley was not on hand, Marian would take a walk and have one of the servants summon her.

She had only glimpsed the library the previous evening. Now, in the clear morning light, she admired its airiness, the soaring shelves of books, the tasteful, muted appointments in gold and deep red. Her eyes found the magnificent marine scene over the hearth.

"'Tis van de Cappelle," Sidley said behind her. As she turned to him, he smiled. "My father had a taste for the Dutch. My grandfather—Well, I saw that you admired the Claude in the dining room last night." When

Marian nodded, he added, "Great-grandfather favored the Italian masters: Caracci, Giotto, Correggio, Titian. . . . You must examine them here at your leisure."

Marian watched as two footmen, bearing between them an easel and several canvases of differing dimension, followed him into the room. A young maid curtsied to Marian before slipping quietly into a seat at the already blazing hearth.

"I would not have you here without a chaperone, Miss Ware," Sidley said as Marian eyed the girl. " 'Tis best to observe the proprieties," he continued, strolling on into the room. "We are like to have spectators enough—I hope you do not mind—though the library is, in the usual course of such a weekend, unfrequented. Literary pursuits seem to coincide with rain." He smiled. "I took the liberty of having some canvas stretched and sized. Mostly half-length . . ." He indicated the supplies that had accompanied him. "But should you prefer your own . . ."

Marian shook her head. "This is more than enough, my lord."

"I knew you would not be traveling with such. And suspected as well that you might have forgotten."

"Forgotten?"

"That you had agreed to paint me."

She thought he was laughing at her. His gaze held something of amusement. He certainly knew that she had never agreed to anything of the sort.

"You have not indicated your own preference in art, my lord."

"Oh, but I have. 'Tis English, and distinctly contemporary."

She looked away from him then, and from his smile, convinced that this exercise in portraiture was part of some elaborate game. "You might have anyone paint you," she said shortly.

"Perhaps. But I am just traditional enough to choose a woman as portraitist when one is available. You must have noticed that Angelica Kauffman painted my grandfather, and Madame Vigée Le Brun, my father." When she nodded, he said pleasantly, "Shall we begin?"

Marian moved toward the windows, sparing only the briefest glance at the view of the park in front with its extensive beds of flowers. When she reached to position a chair to one side of the windows, a footman was there before her to fulfill the task.

"You wish me to sit, then?" Sidley asked.

"To start, my lord. Unless you have something particular in mind?"

"What would you have me tell you, Miss Ware? That I must be posed astride a thundering steed, or strutting with sword aloft?" He laughed at her impatient expression. "I have no preference."

"Then I shall make a few sketches first. I might ask you to stand later."

He nodded. Marian surveyed his elegant but dark attire, noting once more the black ribbon about one sleeve. "You wish to be painted in mourning?"

" 'Twould seem appropriate."

"I thought perhaps your regimentals . . ."

"No." The single word was emphatic.

Marian thought with regret that he must have looked magnificent in uniform.

"May I state a preference, though," she said, "for a coat that is a bit brighter? 'Twould make for a more vibrant painting."

"What color would you like then, Miss Ware?" He was signaling a footman.

"I—one of blue, I think, my lord."

As the footman listened to the order and departed, Sidley looked down at her. "You are fond of blue, Miss Ware?"

"Not overmuch," she assured him. The wretch was too pointedly holding her gaze with the cobalt depth of his own. Opening her sketchbook, she gestured to the chair. "If you would, my lord."

For some minutes she drew in silence as he faced the window. He did not move even when the footman returned with a valet, who carried three coats. In some distraction Marian, who had become absorbed in her work, looked to the servants as the valet cleared his throat.

"You must tell me whether I am permitted to move or speak, Miss Ware," Sidley said, maintaining his pose.

"Oh! Of course, my lord."

He turned to the proffered wardrobe. Marian was not surprised at his choice. She suspected it was the same coat he had worn in Hatchards's two weeks before, when they had been introduced. When he sought her approval, she quickly gave it.

"I shall wear it tomorrow, then," he said to her relief.

For a moment she had wondered if he intended to change right there before her. As she felt her cheeks grow warm, she concentrated on the paper in front of her and asked him once again to look away.

"Are we not to have any conversation then, Miss Ware?" he asked after some time. "I confess I had not planned on so much reflection. If you must know, 'tis a form of penance."

"You might talk if you wish, my lord."

"And you shall dutifully listen?" His lips did not smile, though his voice did. "Can you not work and speak at once?"

"Of course I can." Though she thought her own claim too brave. At that moment she was contemplating the firm lines to his mouth and chin, the way in which the morning light played across his even features. "This is . . . this is a very beautiful room," she said.

"It is perhaps my favorite at Aldersham," he said. "And not only because it is, in general, private. I find it particularly appealing in the morning, and I am by nature an early riser—which will, no doubt, surprise you, Miss Ware."

"Why should that surprise me?"

His lips twitched. "I was under the impression that

you believed my nocturnal entertainments must leave me desperate for sleep, as most of our friends seem to be this morning."

"You might be desperate for sleep, my lord, and still rise early." She suspected that was indeed the case, as she thought again that he looked peaked, much too pale. She heard him mutter "impertinent creature," but the comment sounded cordial enough, and when she asked him to turn to face her, his gaze was steady and open.

"I was used to riding every morning," he told her. "Do you ride, Miss Ware?"

"I have ridden, my lord, but never regularly. For want of a horse."

"You must ride here."

"I shall probably be too busy—with your portrait, my lord."

He smiled. "You needn't work so assiduously. I do not demand too close a likeness."

"I do not see the purpose of a portrait that is not a likeness."

"Which explains why this might be your sole commission, my dear Miss Ware. Few are satisfied with a likeness."

"Is this a commission then, my lord? I had thought perhaps 'twas a favor."

One well-shaped eyebrow rose. "A favor to me, certainly. But no, you will be paid for your time and talent. I am not that mean."

She asked him to stand and face the window.

"What do you think of our company, Miss Ware?"

"It seems a very jolly group."

" 'Jolly'?" The set line to his lips disputed that rather impatiently. "I fear you do not look below the surface. Or perhaps you have not observed much beyond Mr. Richard Poole's smiles?"

Marian frowned. "If you cannot look happy, my lord, I would wish you might at least relax. Your face reflects your thoughts."

"Does it?" He turned to look directly at her. "If so, you must read my mind. You must know what I am thinking this minute."

She thought at first that he was angry; the intensity of his expression made her think so. But there was something else there, something she would most closely liken to hunger.

"You are thinking of your breakfast," she said.

His features relaxed. "Close enough, I suppose, that I must credit you with knowing what you are about." A small smile stayed with him as he again faced the window.

" 'Twas an expression you might not want so accurately portrayed," Marian suggested.

For a moment he was silent. "That would depend, Miss Ware," he told her lightly, "on where the thing is to be displayed."

Again she worked silently, until she asked him to face her while standing.

"What do you think of the ladies, then?" he asked.

"I like them all."

"As do I. But you draw no distinctions?"

"Were I to do so, even with my host," she said with some heat, "I should be thought rude."

He smiled briefly. "Can you picture any of them as mistress of Aldersham?"

"Your aunt, Lady Adeline, certainly."

He laughed. "Touché, Miss Ware."

Marian had to look away from his gaze. She concentrated on his brow and the sculpted line of his cheek.

"You remind me of my old nurse," he said, once again demanding her attention.

"Am I to be complimented, my lord?"

"Never more so! She was the most disciplined person I have ever known. I thought of her often on the Peninsula—to my enduring benefit, I assure you. Discipline saves lives."

Marian, not knowing how to respond, applied herself to her work. When he stood even five feet away, he seemed to loom over her; she thought she must paint him seated, if only for her own peace of mind. She frowned as she considered that—and the idea that he compared her to a martinet of a nurse.

"You are, of course, much younger and prettier."

"My lord, I—"

"And you do not squint."

She choked back a laugh.

"My old nurse, Miss Philomela Philpott—"

"That was not her name!" Marian objected.

"Oh, do you know her, then?"

"Of course not," she protested. "But, my lord, you are absurd!"

He smiled. "Sadly, I never did know Miss Philpott's Christian name. She was above all things proper, and moved on to a worthier youngster almost a score of years ago. At all times I called her merely 'Nurse.' But the point, Miss Ware, is that I shall never forget the last words she said to me. 'Master Leland,' she said—for I was not always Sidley, you understand—'Master Leland, you must keep your affairs in order.' And that is what I have attempted ever since."

Marian drew a rather emphatic line about his collar. "This is true?" she asked.

"Truth matters to you?"

"Why, of course," she said simply, and startled an expression on his face that was uncharacteristically serious.

"The reference," he continued, "was to keeping my affairs in order. For I find that with the passage of time my affairs have multiplied alarmingly. And among them is the need to maintain my family and its standing." He paused. "I must take a wife."

She could not meet his gaze. "I have meant to tell you, my lord, how grateful I am to be included in this party. I know that it is—that I am not—that Katie—"

"It is my pleasure, and my aunt's, to have your company, Miss Ware," he said smoothly. "Your presence would enhance any party."

She raised her chin to stifle the impulse to cry. For the words were at once everything proper, yet distancing all the same. Despite her effort, her lips trembled.

"I fear I must take a break for some minutes here, Miss Ware," he told her as he moved away from the windows, "for I see my steward crossing the lawn, and I must have a word with him. Your pardon."

Marian breathed in relief once he had left the room. His presence made a mockery of her self-control, emphasizing just how alive to him she was. Placing her sketchbook aside, she reached for her painting smock and slid it over her gown. The young maid jumped up to help her tie it in back, before opening one of the windows to admit the morning air. For some minutes Marian debated which of several poses she should paint and settled on having him seated, more for his own comfort with his injured leg than for any preference of her own. This task, which should have been easy, was, in fact, proving arduous.

When a footman arrived with a pot of hot chocolate and two cups upon a tray, Marian had him pour out for her. She savored sips of the heavenly potion as she blocked out the canvas. By the time Sidley returned, she had recovered some level of equanimity.

"I apologize," he told her, taking a seat when she gestured to it. "Just a small matter, but important nonetheless."

Until that moment she had not focused on how many "small matters" must be comprehended in the smooth running of an estate such as Aldersham. Perhaps Lord Sidley was not as inattentive as she had heard, that the place should be so magnificent.

"I see you've sampled the chocolate," he said, having a footman bring him a cup.

"It is delicious," she said. "Most extravagant."

He looked pleased. " 'Tis the French method. I have converted my aunt to it, despite her protests."

"Why should she protest?"

"Lady Adeline believes it intemperate to find too much pleasure in any one thing." His gaze watched her over the rim of his cup. "Do you sympathize with her, Miss Ware?"

"Not at all. I suppose I indulge myself in painting. I should rather paint than anything else. I might spend hours and scarce be conscious of the time."

"It sounds a complete trance."

She thought his tone somewhat dismissive. "I see no call to disparage concentration, my lord."

"I do not 'disparage.' 'Tis envy you hear, Miss Ware."

"Envy?"

"I have only ever found one subject as transfixing."

At his subsequent silence, she peered around the canvas at him. His gaze, his grin, made her blush.

"We speak of different passions, my lord," she said stonily. "My interest is most selective."

"I assure you, Miss Ware, so is mine."

For some time she did not speak to him, except to ask him to lift his chin or shift his shoulders. She hid behind the wall of canvas and let herself believe she disliked him.

"Tell me, what does your Lieutenant Reeves look like?"

The question, coming after a prolonged silence, startled her so much that for a moment she could not even recall William's face.

"He is not as tall as you are, my lord."

"Dwarfish?"

"Certainly not. He is of medium height."

"You think me not 'medium'?"

"You are tall, my lord. You know that you are tall."

"And Lieutenant Reeves' complexion?"

"He is fair. Not as fair as Lord Benjamin—"

"Swarthy?"

"Quite the opposite. He can blush—"

"Good heavens, Miss Ware. What do you say to him to make him blush?"

"I meant only that he is fair-complected."

"And is he hefty?"

" 'Hefty'? I would never describe him so." She found it difficult to picture William while attempting to capture every nuance of Sidley's face. "He is not broad—"

"Thin, then."

"—nor is he thin. You are thinner than he, my lord."

"You mean that he is stout."

"He is not stout! You have been ill. Naturally you appear somewhat thin—"

"I wish you would not continually dwell on my illness, Miss Ware. 'Tis most disheartening."

After the set-down, she chose to be silent.

"And his interests?" Sidley persisted. "I presume he is fond of art."

"He has admired my sketches, yes."

"No doubt he calls them your 'little sketches,'" he said with something of a sneer in his voice.

And Marian, angry because William did indeed refer to her work in that manner, countered, "He has not seen me in more than two years, my lord. He must be forgiven for not . . . for not understanding—"

"You?"

Marian glared at him. "The degree of my commitment," she supplied.

"Yet he asks for your commitment to him."

She drew a deep breath and for a moment concentrated very hard on Lord Sidley's supercilious nose. "I know this is your home, Lord Sidley. And that at the moment I am not quite a guest. I am in your employ—"

"I am your patron, Miss Ware. It is not the same."

"But all the same," she continued, "you overstep. Lieutenant Reeves is none of your affair."

He did not look at her; he managed to look toward her yet through her and to maintain that slight smile upon his lips.

With his stoic silence she painted then at a furious pace, feeling equally furious with herself for believing that in speaking so, *she* might have overstepped. And when her aunt joined them, Marian took the opportunity to release him from his pose until the morrow, though she did not anticipate that Lord Sidley should ever wish to renew the process.

"This is very good of you, Marian," Edith said, moving to her side to review the painting's beginning.

" 'Tis not 'very good of' me, Aunt, when the project was unavoidable. I could not very well deny our host."

"And so it is very good of you, my dear," Edith repeated equably. "What has overset you so? You are usually happiest to be painting anything. And this has started very well indeed."

"I intend to finish it as though demons pursued me, Edith. For he is the most—most *insufferable* sitter! Presumptuous and suggestive and—Oh! I vow I am tempted to do something dreadful to his likeness, would it not reflect poorly on you and Katie and Edgar."

Edith smiled. "But I know you will do a most superior portrait, no matter the provocation, Marian, because that is your nature. You must not let him trouble you; I am convinced he merely teases. We've only a few days, after all. And I doubt he shall concern himself in the slightest, even if you should choose never to finish the painting."

Marian stopped to stare at her. "Do you truly think so? However eccentric he may sound on occasion, I believe Lord Sidley is quite serious about a number of matters. His portrait, for one—whether *I* complete something he approves or not. And for another, he is most serious about marriage."

Edith drew a breath. "Oh, Marian—did he mention Katie?"

"He did not, Aunt," she said, instantly regretting that temper had loosened her tongue. "He said only that he must wed."

Edith's brow furrowed. "Adeline has been telling me she expects him to decide rather soon. I fear—I fear, Marian, that he may be more taken with Miss Tinckney-Dwight than our Katie."

"Katie might be better out of it," Marian countered grimly, brushing paint unsparingly onto the canvas. "Do you truly think she would be happy with a man like Lord Sidley?"

"There are few like Lord Sidley, Marian," Edith said with a smile. "But Katie is still an impressionable girl. She admires the man; in time she might learn true affection. He is not inattentive or cruel. Where is the want of happiness in that?"

When Edith left, Marian silently continued her work, so dedicated was she to accomplishing as much of the piece as possible in the shortest time. But her aunt's question reminded her too acutely of her own qualms with regard to William. And when she broke to join the rest of the party at a late breakfast, she knew she was far from satisfied with what had comprised nearly four hours of effort.

Lord Sidley, still in his dark coat but sporting high spirits, entertained all of them during the meal, then organized an outing to the local fair. Since Katie had suggested the visit, Edith considered Sidley's ready compliance a sign of his regard for her daughter. But Marian, observing her host as he escorted Katie and Delia to one of several carriages, was convinced otherwise.

Their caravan joined a stream of other vehicles toward the grounds of the annual fair at Turling, where booths and tents displayed a variety of goods and entertainments. Given the town's proximity to London and other market centers, the merchandise tended more to the fresh or the amusing, since people had access to many of the necessities at any other time. Nonetheless, livestock dealers vied for attention with traders in a wide range of goods, while balladeers and musicians serenaded all attending. Marian enjoyed watching a puppet show with her cousins, visiting a conjurer with the Pooles, nibbling tasty gingerbread and buying a few locally crafted gifts for friends and family.

She had been walking with the Pooles, when Dicky left them briefly to speak to a neighbor with regard to purchasing a horse.

Clara turned to her with a smile. "Your cousin, Lady Katherine, is a most spirited young lady. She must be very popular in town."

"I believe she is, Miss Poole. She has always enjoyed company and maintains a large circle of acquaintance."

"Does she share your artistic interests, Miss Ware?"

Marian laughed and shook her head. "She appreciates fine things, Miss Poole. And Katie has an excellent eye for detail. Her memory for dress and décor is truly remarkable. I find we complement each others' deficits in observation."

"You are very fond of your cousin."

"Yes. Yes, I am."

"Then I think, Miss Ware—I think you'd best pre-pare her. Lord Sidley is unlikely to let affection dictate his choice."

Affection! For Katie? As Marian watched Sidley tilt his dark head toward Katie's beribboned bonnet, her first thought was that his indulgence should never be inter-preted as affection or even a particular regard. But she soon realized that Clara Poole was telling her some-thing else entirely, and in as kind a manner as possible.

"You have Lord Sidley's confidence?" she asked.

"My brother and I have been close to the family for many years, Miss Ware. I know I risk—I risk sounding presumptuous. But I mean only to help. I should hate to think your cousin's expectations were to be frustrated. I do not know her heart."

"Whom has he—whom has he chosen?" Marian asked, with a sick dread weighing upon her chest.

"I cannot know for certain. But Dicky and I believe he will determine, logically and perhaps unfortunately, that Miss Tinckney-Dwight suits his interests."

Marian stayed with Clara Poole as they visited the stalls of cloth merchants, furriers, candle and soap mak-ers, and at last a hawker of wonderfully carved and painted wooden toys. Marian's attention fixed on a charming, standing cat, holding a tiny brush, that would, upon pressing a button, turn repeatedly between a small palette and an easel holding a painting of three kittens. But though Clara Poole urged her to purchase the toy, Marian was no longer in any mood to be entertained. They joined the rest of the party outside a fortune-teller's tent.

"I would have all my guests submit," Lord Sidley bid them, gesturing the ladies inside, "as I have one task yet to accomplish. At supper this evening I expect to hear the prediction for each of you."

"But what of you, Sidley?" Lord Benjamin asked with a laugh, "Are we to create yours?"

"I know my fortune, Benny. Repeating it scarcely improves it. You must put in a good word for me." And he departed, with the claim that he needed to engage two new boys for Aldersham's stables.

Marian watched him go with a sense of resignation. He had not looked her way once all afternoon. Though that was for the best, she found she could not like it. Her misery increased when Delia Tinckney-Dwight smiled at her.

"Do come sit with me, Miss Ware," she said politely. "I am convinced that some of your bright prospects must in close quarters benefit my own."

And as they entered the dim sanctuary of the fortune-teller's tent, Marian wished she did not find Delia half so nice.

Chapter Seven

T hey were late back from the fair, but a festive dinner awaited them, and Lady Adeline and Lady Formsby, who had not accompanied them on the expedition, wished to hear all about the afternoon's outing.

Marian noted that the seating arrangements had been carefully altered, such that Katie still sat next to Sidley, but on his left, and Becca Harvey had moved to his right. Delia Tinckney-Dwight now found her place at the center of the table, and Marian and Clara were shifted that much farther from their host, to the end over which Lady Adeline presided.

Marian liked Lady Adeline. Thus she could not quite understand her discomfort around her hostess, who was such a close friend of her cousin Edith. But there was something a bit too assessing in the older woman's gaze, something Marian deemed too closely observant and not altogether warm. She suspected that Lady Adeline guessed at her attraction to Lord Sidley.

"So, Miss Ware," she said now rather abruptly, and speaking across Sir Philip, who sat between them, "would you ever find an event such as the humble Turling fair worthy of a painting?"

"Indeed I would, my lady. Had I thought to take my sketchbook, I suspect I'd have spent less time on purchases."

"Do you never draw from memory?"

"On occasion, certainly, ma'am. But there is something less . . . immediate, I suppose, about the result. I must make an effort to remember what I've seen, and I fear the labor shows."

Lady Adeline's gaze appeared to soften. "My family has always admired the arts. I myself was very fond of drawing when I was younger."

"I should like to see some of your drawings."

But her hostess waved the suggestion aside. "Mere scribbles, I assure you, Miss Ware. Suitable only for prompting those few memories I retain."

"I will not grant you any deficiency in memory, Lady Adeline," Sir Philip said gallantly.

"You have no notion, sir, of how many years I am ahead of you! But your flattery is welcome nonetheless."

As the two bantered, Marian turned to her right, to Mr. Harvey. She had found him to be a very good, forthright sort of man; he reminded her of the earnest shopkeepers and gentlemen farmers at her home in Brinford. Except, of course, that they could not claim to have earned even a fraction of Mr. Harvey's fortune.

He had been talking about his Becca, of her precocious ability with horses as a youngster and the splash she had created in town that season. His ambition for his daughter was quite as plain as his affection. Now he glanced to the other end of the table.

"You have an artist's eye, Miss Ware—do you not think they look well together?" he asked.

And Marian was compelled to look toward Sidley, whose dark head was at that moment inclined to catch something Becca Harvey said.

"Yes," she agreed softly, though in truth she thought any of the young ladies under consideration would look well with Lord Sidley.

Her gaze lingered too long. When Sidley broke his conversation with a smile and glanced down the table, his own gaze fastened on hers. Despite the smile, there was such intensity in his look that Marian quickly withdrew her own. She mumbled some further meaningless assent to Mr. Harvey, then played with her silver as he described his visits to several counties in search of a suitable property to acquire.

As the course was removed, Sidley asked broadly of the table, "When shall I have my report? Am I to believe in the old woman's divinations after all?"

Several people responded at once.

But Katie, seated next to him, claimed his ear. "Well, my lord," she said boldly, "I was promised a handsome husband."

Given Katie's accompanying arch look, Marian feared she might choke. Indeed, she heard Edith's sharply indrawn breath.

But Lord Sidley looked unfazed. "We might well believe that prophecy, Lady Katherine," he said blandly. "Your suitor is to be congratulated."

While Katie looked happily undaunted, he turned to Becca Harvey. "Is Lady Katherine unique, Miss Harvey, or did our canny Cassandra promise you the same?"

Becca shook her chestnut head. "My fortune was quite different, Lord Sidley. She told me she saw 'fast horses and a long journey.' "

"Certainly you must welcome the prospect of fast horses," Sidley said. "Given your equestrian talents."

"Oh, always, my lord."

"No one rides as well as Miss Harvey," Edgar enthused, drawing a black look from Lord Benjamin.

"But the rest makes little sense, my lord," her father pointed out, "as we're only a day from town, as are all the estates I'm reviewing."

"Perhaps what seems 'long' to such an elderly woman is only a day's journey for your fast horses, Mr. Harvey," Sidley said.

"There is that, my lord! If you are determined to make sense of what isn't."

Sidley smiled. "My skepticism prompts this review, sir," he said, "yet you find me too gullible?"

"Ah, no, my lord, that was not my meaning."

"Did you have your palm read, Mr. Harvey?"

"I did. All the woman said was 'timely assistance.' Timely assistance! If anyone can make heads or tails of that."

Mrs. Harvey chirped in, "She told me I shall have a magnificent new hat, my lord!"

"That I must believe, ma'am," Sidley said with a nod to her, "as the bonnet and its bearer must always suit."

Mrs. Harvey actually blushed with pleasure.

"You will appreciate my reading, Sidley," Lord Benjamin volunteered. "She told me I would make a fortunate investment."

"A 'fortunate investment,' Benny, might mean gaining hundreds of pounds or merely one."

"All the more reason to wager hundreds!"

"But remark, my friend. She referred only to *an* investment, not *all*. She did not indicate which. I fear your probabilities have not altered in the slightest."

"Possibly not! But it certainly makes me *feel* lucky!"

Sidley shook his head and looked to Edgar. "Lord Formsby, did you submit?"

"I did, Sidley. I was told I shall come into a fine property. But since I already *have* a fine property, I don't very well know what that might mean."

"I should think marriage," Sir Philip remarked. " 'Tis

the accepted way, for one of your age. No guessing there, I imagine!"

"I hadn't really thought," Edgar said. But his gaze traveled to Becca Harvey, causing Marian to trade looks with Edith across the table.

"You are to be congratulated," Lord Sidley told Edgar, "but this is not enough to qualify as soothsaying. At your age, as Sir Philip mentioned, a young man might be presumed to be contemplating matrimony."

"Even men a bit older might contemplate it," Lady Adeline observed equably.

"Indeed, Aunt. Sir Philip, was such a proposition put to you?"

Sir Philip laughed. "An end to my widowed status was not discussed, my lord. Quite the contrary. I was told that my *grandchildren* would adore me."

"Papa, she didn't!" his daughter protested.

"She did, m'dear," he assured Delia with a wink.

"Might we make an assumption regarding your own future then, Miss Tinckney-Dwight?" Sidley paired the question with such a warm smile that Marian feared a proposal was imminent.

"I was promised a contented household, my lord. Children spoiled by my father might not further such contentment."

The comment drew laughter from the entire table.

Really, Marian thought in some despair, *Delia is quite perfect for him. Perhaps they will announce before the visit ends.* And beneath the table her hands tightened into fists.

"Clara Poole," Sidley tasked her, "what did our old friend have to tell you?"

"I fear she was most general, most vague, Lee. She told me I shall be loved."

"That is not the future, Clara. That is the present."

She acknowledged the comment with a shy smile.

"Our 'old friend,' as you term her, Sidley," Dicky said, "is clearly tired of *me.* She tells me the same every year—that I shall marry a 'good' woman and become fat. I cannot determine if I am to marry a cook or be so pestered for my sins, I turn to sweets for solace!"

In the midst of the subsequent laughter, Sidley made sport of sighing loudly. "I perceive the trend. Our palmist always speaks the same. She is predictable as the sunrise, possibly because she is two hundred years old. Certainly her tattered cloak looks as though a cavalier gifted it to her."

"Sidley!" his aunt protested. "The woman was a girl when I was."

"Was she, Auntie? My deepest apologies. But we must still conclude that the young woman foretells love, wealth, and happiness with reliable consistency. No one has been delivered of a sad or even an uncertain fate."

"Oh, but Marian was," Katie promptly supplied. "She was told she will be 'crossed in love.' "

As Marian felt all eyes on her, she looked to Katie in some exasperation.

But once again Sidley drew her attention. "Is that so?" he asked.

She thought his hooded gaze calculating.

"I can only believe that would be the case, Miss Ware, if you were to give your heart to the undeserving."

No, Marian denied silently, looking at him. *Not undeserving. But perhaps, in this instance, unfeeling.*

"Lieutenant Reeves is most deserving, my lord," Edith said.

"Then perhaps we've discovered a fault in our forecaster's record. Did she say nothing else, Miss Ware?"

Marian knew he would have all from her—at any cost.

"Her precise words, my lord," she relayed distinctly, "were: 'This lady will be crossed in love but will find much favor.' "

"Ah! Then she sugared her reading with something positive. Perhaps you will find that your love was rather a fragile thing, to be 'crossed' at all."

"Sidley!" his aunt objected once more. "Miss Ware's affections could only ever be sincere."

"My apologies, Miss Ware." He condescended to nod to Marian. "You mustn't take my words amiss. Naturally, if one is to be 'crossed in love,' 'tis the other party's sincerity that should be questioned."

"Sidley!" Lady Adeline repeated.

This time the rest of the table was silent for some rather painful seconds, a silence broken by Lord Vaughn. He grinned at Marian, who sat across from him. "I believe I must rob you of the award for the worst fortune, Miss Ware. I was informed I would find 'peace in purpose'—as enigmatic a prospect as Sidley might hope for. I deduce that unless I am meant to purchase colors once more, I must take other 'orders' and enter the church."

"Nonsense!" Lord Benjamin cried over the light, nervous laughter of some at the table. "I suspect instead you are intended to tell old 'Gruff'un' Knox—"

"Benny," Sidley interrupted sharply, "I recall you promised to partner Miss Harvey at cards tonight, did you not? As it is already late, I suggest we remove ourselves to that pleasure. I sense that Miss Harvey grows impatient."

"Not at all, Lord Sidley," Becca said, though she rose from her seat at almost the same instant as Lady Adeline rose from hers. "And you have not told us why you never seek your own fortune."

"Because I prefer not to know any of it, Miss Harvey. Blindness to one's fate lends a man a decided advantage. Had I known what was to befall me the past dozen years, I might not have weathered them half as well."

At this his friends teased him, but Marian was led to reflect. Her cousin Edith, perhaps judging incorrectly that Marian was troubled by her projected fate, squeezed her arm solicitously as they removed to the drawing room. But it was Lord Sidley's future that troubled Marian, not her own.

He had hired a quartet of musicians, which now serenaded them at cards. The extravagance of bringing such a group from town amazed Marian; no doubt they were originally intended to play for Aldersham's guests at dancing, as Sidley had hinted the previous evening.

Marian glanced over at his table, where he partnered Delia against the Harveys. He was at ease and smiling; the lantern light made his jet hair shine. He looked as though he hadn't a care in the world. Yet someone, and Marian suspected Lord Sidley himself, had placed Marian at cards with Lord Benjamin, Edgar, and Becca Harvey. The jealously competitive undercurrents among such a threesome ensured that Marian's usual dislike for card games was even more pronounced. She had to wonder why she alone drew such dedicated, discomfiting attention from their congenial host.

When Rebecca Harvey, claiming a headache, begged off extending the evening, Marian happily followed the girl's lead in seeking dismissal. She had been awake early, and the afternoon had been a long one. And she knew she must once again paint Sidley in the morning—a prospect that she could not entirely welcome.

Had Sidley not proposed the project in portraiture himself, he'd have likened it to some form of torture. Certainly its novelty had faded by the close of the previous day's session. This morning's sitting would necessarily be shorter, since he'd promised to take much of the party on a tour of the park, with an extended stop for a picnic. He accepted the sitting's curtailment with considerable relief, knowing that he could not be trusted with

Miss Ware. His comments the previous evening had been proof enough of that. His own unreasoned behavior had appalled him.

His aunt had not yet spoken to him, but her looks had served. He anticipated her disapproving presence in the library this morning.

Grimly, he donned the blue coat that Marian Ware had preferred. He knew his vanity, his despicable vanity, had led him to seek what he should not have sought from the girl, to test a commitment that had clearly been tested enough during the two-year absence of her fiancé.

Vaughn, charging that Sidley was "not acting as he ought," no longer spoke to him, and Dicky Poole had sent him too many questioning looks. Soon his genteel neighbors, the Pooles, would comprehend just how inanely their old friend Sidley was behaving.

Yet she was here, in his home, and he could picture no other woman in it as long as she remained.

"Deuce take it," he muttered as his valet straightened the coat and brushed a small sprinkling of powder from one sleeve. Sidley was wearing less powder; he was determined to "recover" in rapid time. But he could not simply stroll into breakfast one morning with a brilliant complexion. The transition had to be accomplished with a modicum of finesse. By the time he returned to town, within the next week or ten days, all would know that Lord Sidley had gained a reprieve.

He picked up the small wooden toy he had purchased the previous afternoon. The trinket had caught his eye as he made his way to the hiring halls; he'd convinced himself Miss Ware deserved it as a token of appreciation. He suspected he would have difficulty enough in settling a reasonable payment on the girl. She was likely to balk at even the most trivial of sums. Miss Ware needed a deputy; she needed someone more responsible than Formsby to forward her affairs. He doubted a newly decommissioned naval lieutenant, one who wished to retire to the country, would answer.

Impatiently he made his way to the library, to discover she was not yet down. He ordered tea instead of chocolate. Yesterday's offering had been intended to seduce, but it had seemed to work its spell solely upon himself. This morning he wished only to get on with the business.

"Oh!"

He heard her behind him. Turning from consideration of the front garden, he confronted her startled expression.

"I—I believed I was early and would precede you, my lord."

"We are all scheduled for a picnic today, Miss Ware." He knew he sounded chilly, decidedly unlike a host happily contemplating a picnic. All the more chilly, perhaps, because he thought she looked rather adorable, somehow particularly so, enveloped as she was in her serviceable painting smock.

"'Tis an energetic enterprise, my lord. You are feeling well enough . . . ?"

"I know my own strength, Miss Ware."

"Certainly." She moved quickly toward her easel. "We shall start at once. If you would kindly—" She broke off as she noticed the toy. "The cat." She took it up and, as though she could not help herself, pressed the button for its operation. Then she turned to him. "Miss Poole must have told you?"

"Clara? Told me what, Miss Ware?"

"Of my interest in the toy. That I admired it."

"Did you admire it? I had no notion. When I saw it, I thought only that you *might* admire it. Clara did not betray your confidences."

"I see." She placed it carefully upon a side table, as though she never intended to take it up again.

"It is a gift, Miss Ware," he said. "In partial payment for this portrait." She was looking as serious as he felt; the atmosphere needed lightening. He forced a smile. "I am gratified to have chosen something you liked."

"Indeed yes. I—thank you, my lord."

He took a seat as the tea arrived. He earnestly set about posing once more.

"Did you—did you review the start of the painting, my lord?"

"No, Miss Ware." He had quite pointedly not done so. He was already reasonably tired of himself. "I needn't see it at all until it satisfies you."

She frowned at that. "I merely wished you to know that I have no preference for concealment while it progresses, as some artists do. You must feel free to comment."

"I trust you, Miss Ware." He turned his gaze briefly to the garden. "The light is not as good this morning."

"It does not matter," she said. He could tell her mind was already engaged with the problem presented. "I remember."

"Perhaps you do not need me at all, then."

"I remember the light, my lord, not your nose."

"How chastening."

"Unless you wish to be painted so, you must not grin."

He corrected his expression. "My aunt threatens to visit us this morning," he said. "I hope you do not mind?"

"Far from it. I enjoy her company. She told us last night at dinner of some of her travels on the Continent when she was younger. She was able to tour for the greater part of a year. How thrilling to see the Alps, Vesuvius, and the Bay of Naples—Rome, Venice, and Athens! I should love it above all things."

"Above all things?" he quizzed. "Assuredly only if Lieutenant Reeves were to accompany you?"

She did not respond, but worked in silence.

"It was a different age, Miss Ware," he commented. "But now, perhaps, likely to return, in some form, with Bonaparte's absence. Europe will once again be open to the pursuit of something other than war. An artist such as yourself should not be deprived of the Grand Tour."

"I am most unlikely to take the Grand Tour, but *a* tour might be possible—someday." Again she worked in silence.

"You have an advantage over the rest of us, an advantage of which I suspect you are scarcely aware. You might make your own tour whenever you wish—paint summer in winter, winter in summer. I think you do not recognize your own power."

"Anyone of imagination has such power."

"Most of us do not summon it with facility, Miss Ware. And I confess to having met with a notable lack of imagination in many fields. Thus we must enliven our walls with the result of *your* imagination, when we have none of our own."

"You do not strike me as unimaginative, my lord."

"Thank you."

"And as for portraiture, I believe it is perhaps better that I not apply my imagination, lest I fail to produce something recognizable."

He laughed. "I see we return to the same topic." He was amazed that she was managing to paint anything at all, recognizable or not. He was exquisitely conscious of her gaze. He found it strangely mesmerizing, as a contented cat must experience a caress. Yet he sensed that her appraisal was elusively impersonal. She was not as affected as he.

"I did not ask—if you have studied portraiture?" He thought his own voice sounded hoarse.

" 'Tis a bit late to ask me that! You did press me into service." When he smiled, she added, "I have studied and practiced portraits, my lord. Enough to know 'tis quite accepted to include something of particular meaning to the sitter, some item of personal significance, in such a study. Should you like your cane, perhaps, or a book or object you admire?"

He shook his head. " 'Tis significant enough that I sit in Aldersham's library. But if you wish, you must devise something, Miss Ware, so that a century hence viewers might say 'There it is! Ware's little joke on Sidley.' " Her smile pleased him so much that he added generously, "As long as you are not cruel, I leave you to it."

"It is a bit late now, my lord. I am locked into this composition. But I shall see." Again she painted silently for some minutes. "Your aunt is a very handsome woman."

"She will be flattered to hear it."

"She must have heard it before."

"One can never hear it enough, Miss Ware. Though it is curious—one rarely terms a woman 'handsome' in her hearing. Women prefer to be called *pretty, charming, elegant, attractive,* or a host of other adjectives."

"Yet *handsome* is strong and lasting. Enduring. Lady Adeline will still draw attention twenty years from now."

"She certainly *commands* attention," he admitted wryly. "But *handsome* does not charm."

"I would debate you, my lord. Its charm is simply more mature. Yes, *handsome* does command. It implies a certain . . . power. Physical, mental, even spiritual." She was at ease, speaking as she painted. He could not take his gaze from the sweeps of her brush behind the canvas. "I've never heard young children described as handsome," she mused aloud, "though a family might be. As a grouping, a family holds strength."

"I confess"—he cleared his throat—"I've never reflected on the term so completely, Miss Ware. But you have persuaded me. I concede that my aunt is *handsome*."

Again they were silent.

"Miss Tinckney-Dwight is certainly very handsome," she said.

"She is. I presume you have considered each member of our little party as potential subject matter."

"I am not so coldly assessing, my lord," she objected, refusing to look at him.

"Then why should you single out Miss Delia for your consideration?"

"I do not 'single her out.' I merely believe her to be an excellent example of *handsome*."

"More so than your own cousin?"

"Katie is widely acknowledged to be beautiful, my lord. But I have never heard her described as handsome."

"It is a function of age."

"I have just explained why I think it is not."

"And why does the difference concern you at all, Miss Ware, as—by your own admission—you are only ever interested in your art?"

"I have never made such an assertion!" She glared at him from the side of the canvas. "And I have many other interests."

"But you do not pursue them."

"Perhaps not routinely. Perhaps not as thoroughly—"

"What interests you, then, Miss Ware, that you do not pursue—thoroughly?"

When she stared at him, with much anger and something else equally unsettling in her expression, he recalled his promise to himself and instantly attempted an apology. "Please do excuse me, Miss Ware," he said, rising from his seat. "I had no thought to needle you so. I—"

"My lord, please sit down. I should very much like to finish with you here this morning."

At which he sat and tried not to look as he felt, which was suddenly, blazingly, angry—whether at her or himself, he could not have said.

"This is why gentlemen do not sit in the presence of ladies, Miss Ware," he attempted. " 'Tis not so much a courtesy as denial of an advantage." When she met the observation with continued silence, he determined to match her for taciturnity. He sat wordless for innumerable minutes.

"Are you wearing powder, my lord?"

The question so startled him that he was slow to respond. She had already abandoned her palette and moved out from behind the canvas to approach him. As she leaned closer to examine his face, he felt her perusal almost as a touch.

"I would ask you not to wear any powder tomorrow morning," she said. "I must see your complexion. Whatever your—whatever scars you may wish to hide—"

"I am not hiding scars, Miss Ware."

"All the more reason, then, not to—"

"Do not stand so close."

She pulled back abruptly. He read her bewilderment in her gaze. But she was continuing to hold and assess his own, which would not do. He was conscious as he had never been before of the presence of the servants.

"And my eyes are blue," he snapped. "As you've had occasion to remark. They have not changed."

With her beautiful lips set grimly, she returned to her post behind the easel, and Sidley at last drew breath.

"You two certainly keep farmers' hours," his aunt remarked from the doorway. "I confess I did not expect such predawn application, even from you, Sidley. Can you paint him in the dark, Miss Ware?"

Marian smiled as his aunt came closer, to stand examining the canvas.

"This is astonishing, my dear," she said. "You have done so much in only two mornings?"

"I work quickly when I have had time to consider the subject, my lady."

"You have thought about me, then, Miss Ware?" Sidley asked.

"I have had time to think about *painting* you, Lord Sidley," she corrected him.

Lady Adeline laughed. "You are not accustomed to such set-downs, Nephew." Her gaze again sought the painting. "You have caught that look, Miss Ware. I had wondered if you would."

" 'Tis difficult to miss, my lady."

"What look?" Sidley asked.

"You shouldn't need it described to you, Sidley," Lady Adeline told him. "All the rest of us are far too familiar with it." She ignored his frown and turned to Marian's paints. "You do not mix much here, Miss Ware, and seem to use a most limited palette."

Marian smiled. "It is my habit, ma'am. As paints are expensive, and the tinting takes time each evening, I extend from few colors."

"It appears to work well, my dear."

"Is my face blue, then, Miss Ware?"

" 'Twill be red, Sidley, once you see what a fine job she has done." Lady Adeline smiled as she looked at Marian. "I confess, I had no idea you were quite so accomplished, having studied in town only a month. What other training had you?"

"Since my childhood, ma'am, I have belonged to a sketching club in Northampton, and my father used to take me painting with him in his last years, after his—after he returned from the Army. As an artillery officer he was well versed in illustration. Then at school, with Lady Katherine, we had drawing and painting. And I have worked at copying for a local printer and engraver."

"Still, it is remarkable, at your age. I hope you needn't abandon it."

"Abandon it, ma'am?"

"Once you are wed."

"Oh, but I have no intention—"

"Little ones are likely to alter your intention."

Marian's cheeks warmed. "I shall always paint, ma'am."

"Ha!" Sidley remarked.

"Do be quiet, Sidley. Should Miss Ware take a disgust of you at this point, where would you be?"

"Without a nose?" he suggested.

"She has, most generously, already graced you with a fine one." She frowned at him. "Why you should initiate this project, Nephew, with the intention of sabotaging it, distracting Miss Ware in such a manner—"

"If anything distracts, ma'am, it is your own charming presence. We made progress enough before you decided to quiz Miss Ware."

Lady Adeline's chin rose. "I must leave you in any event," she said. "Edith and I shall accompany you on your picnic today, Sidley. I would speak with you before we depart."

"Certainly, Aunt. In fact"—he rose from his chair—"do forgive me, Miss Ware, but I find I grow a bit stiff, settled here so long."

"I am sorry, my lord. I should have thought—"

"He is most capable of looking after himself, Miss Ware," Lady Adeline observed. "You must not apologize."

Sidley smiled. "No indeed," he said. "Far be it from

me to oppose any lady's efforts on my behalf. My wishes must always parallel her own."

At which his aunt pursed her lips and made for the door.

"Miss Ware, please excuse me," Sidley said. "You have enough to get on here this morning?"

Marian nodded and watched him follow his aunt. As the two departed, she heard Sidley say, "Tomorrow. I promise," before the doors clicked shut behind them.

Chapter Eight

Later that afternoon, Marian sat sketching by Aldersham's picturesquely placed lake. Her thoughts returned repeatedly to the assurance she had overheard Sidley give his aunt; she puzzled unhappily over his reference to "tomorrow" and feared he meant to select a bride at any moment. In the hour's repose after their picnic, Marian had watched him escort the party's eligible damsels in strolls about the serene water—first Becca Harvey, then Katie, and now Delia Tinckney-Dwight. Marian believed the purpose of the exercise only too obvious.

She sketched studiously, trying to force her attention to Aldersham's lovely expanses or to the idle conversation about her. The remaining picnickers had settled lazily under the trees, in various states of awareness. Miss Poole and her brother had stayed close to Marian and now commented intermittently on aspects of the landscape or the neighborhood. Lady Adeline and Edith sat together some few feet away. Though at times they spoke quietly, their gazes pointedly followed Sidley and his companion on each of his rounds. After her own outing, Katie sat beside her mother and sipped lemonade as she also quietly assessed Sidley's activity.

Lord Vaughn had accompanied Becca Harvey on a ride with Edgar and Lord Benjamin, no doubt intending to keep the peace among the trio. And while her husband dozed peacefully near the emptied picnic hampers, Mrs. Harvey breathlessly fed *on dit*s from town to an obligingly receptive Sir Philip.

As Marian's gaze again drifted to the couple circling the lake, she likened Sidley's effort to a ritual. She turned a page in her sketchbook with some vigor, only to have Dicky Poole note the action.

"Before you begin another, Miss Ware, might I convince you to take a walk about the lake? I, at least, must work up an appetite for the next meal."

Marian smiled but shook her head and retained her sketchbook. She wished to finish her private depiction of Sidley, as they had only the next day before returning to town.

"Then I propose to take a solo jaunt," Dicky said, rising to his feet. "I shall move clockwise, to confront our host head-on. His measured method wears." Which comment told Marian that Dicky had also noted Sidley's regimen.

As Dicky strode on down the slope toward the lake, Clara smiled at Marian. "My brother's spirits have lifted here at Aldersham," she remarked, her fond gaze on Dicky's tousled brown head. "I'm much relieved. I know my own low mood has weighed on him. I have been the poorest company."

"That is most doubtful," Marian said, returning the smile. "You have been the best of company here, though your situation is one that all of us would find difficult." As Clara swallowed, Marian risked a question. "Were they much alike, Lord Sidley and his brother?"

Clara sighed as her gaze moved to Sidley and Delia across the water.

"They *looked* much alike, though Simon was not as dark—his hair was closer in color to Dicky's. And he was always more reserved than Lee, less . . . , playful, perhaps. He was at all times aware that he was heir to Aldersham. I think he felt more keenly the responsibility to the family, with his father so distracted by Lady Sidley's difficulties, and having a younger brother. I have wondered if that is why he chose to run off to war there at the end. 'Twas the only irresponsible thing Simon ever did. The future, even . . . even with me, must have seemed much too settled. And despite our attachment, he'd convinced himself I was still too young to wed. I shall be twenty this autumn, Miss Ware," she added.

In the subsequent pause, Marian reflected that in this

group of very young women, she herself was one of the eldest. Only Delia Tinckney-Dwight claimed some two additional years.

"Simon and Lee were always close," Clara continued. "They loved their mother dearly, but she was never—never quite to rights. Luckily, her sons were not troubled in that particular way. Always very steady and strong."

Dicky Poole was making quick work of the distance to the other couple. As he at last saluted Sidley and bowed with a comically low flourish to Delia, Marian kept her gaze on them rather than Clara.

"It must be doubly hard, then, that Lord Sidley should be so ill now."

"He *was* ill, Miss Ware. But you see how much improved he looks here at home. Even at breakfast I noticed that his color was much healthier."

Marian hated to correct the girl, to disillusion her. And, truth be told, Lord Sidley *had* looked better today than yesterday. Perhaps excitement regarding his decision had given him a beneficial glow. Or he had removed some powder.

"You know him best, Miss Poole," she conceded, pressing her pencil point too darkly against the page. "And certainly we must always hope. But you must be aware of the talk—that his condition is most serious. . . ."

"*Lee* has said so?"

"I think—well, I do not quite know. But Lady Adeline

is very close to my aunt Edith. She would have relayed anything to the contrary."

"I do not believe it!" Clara objected. "If that is the talk, there is some misapprehension. We heard he was ill on returning to England. We heard he had come near to losing his leg. Lady Adeline was most distraught. But he was always strong. If anything, the years away have only made him more so. True, when he arrived last week, we were told that an accident in town had set him back"—Marian had the grace to blush guiltily—"but he's threatened that tonight he means to dance! And Dicky expects to go riding with him any day. Lee is not foolishly impetuous, Miss Ware. He would not attempt so much unprepared."

"Then perhaps we have been misinformed," Marian allowed. She did not have the heart to discourage her. She could not meet Clara Poole's frown and returned diligently to the complexities of her sketch.

"Indeed, I must believe so. Else why should he be contemplating marriage?"

"We—we understood he thought it time," Marian said. "Regardless of his—regardless of his prospects."

When she again looked up, Clara's expression was more contemplative than alarmed. She was watching the three now ambling along the lakeside toward them.

"Tell me, Miss Ware, what do you think of Miss Tinckney-Dwight?"

"I think"—Marian still concentrated on her pencil strokes—"that she is quite . . . perfect."

"Yes," Clara sighed beside her. "It is impossible not to find her so. And yet . . . But he must know his own mind."

Marian at last looked up. "You do not object—that Lord Sidley appears to have chosen?"

Clara shook her head, though her small smile was rueful. "Dicky and I wish him happy. Lee is in many ways another brother. We must welcome his choice as we would welcome any member of the family."

The words were generous; they were proper. But despite the acceptance of Delia's perfections, Marian sensed a certain disappointment. Whether it was on Clara's part or Sidley's, Marian did not press. She had come to an understanding of her own, an understanding that at once dismayed her and led her to take care with Clara Poole's feelings. In observing Sidley that afternoon, Marian had realized that she could not proceed with her engagement to William Reeves, that she could not bind herself to a marriage of practicality alone. However ill-fated the choice, however improper the sentiment, she was in love with another; she was in love with Lord Sidley.

She had not believed hearts such weak instruments, to be drawn so easily and completely from their own safe interest. Yet hers had proved remarkably, traitorously adaptable. And she would soon find herself in Clara Poole's unenviable position, but without the open acknowledgment of bereavement.

She could no longer work and sat scribbling upon the page in some agitation.

"Ho!" Dicky called as the walkers approached. "We must make haste for the domicile. Sidley insists we dance this evening."

Katie had discarded her lemonade and now rose to join them. "Will we have the same musicians, my lord?" she asked, inserting herself neatly between Sidley and Delia.

"We will indeed, Lady Katherine. And they will play whatever tune you request." Sidley's gaze fell upon Marian's sketch, which she hurriedly covered. "How industrious you are, Miss Ware. You put the rest of our frolicking party to shame."

"You have been a most industrious walker, my lord."

His smile was irritatingly satisfied. "I have, haven't I? After such rigorous exercise, Lady Katherine's gigue will no doubt be beyond me."

"Oh, no!" Katie protested. "I shall ask them to play it slowly!"

"A dirge of a gigue? I am most grateful, my lady."

Marian suspected that only she noticed the challenge in Sidley's voice. She knew it annoyed him to be treated as an invalid.

"You must have them play everything slowly, Lady Katherine," Dicky said. "I have not been dancing for many months and must consult the steps cards."

"I shall show you this afternoon if you like," Katie offered helpfully. "And this evening you might dance with Marian, for she was always termed patient by our dancing instructor."

"Was she indeed?" Dicky asked with a smile. "I should have wished to dance with Miss Ware in any event."

"Are we ready to return?" Sidley asked abruptly. "Lady Formsby, have you had quite enough of the air? Auntie?"

They piled into the carriages for the brief drive back, leaving servants to pack up the remains of their repast and direct the riding party home. Most then retreated to their rooms for a period of rest before the evening's entertainments. Indeed, Katie actually slept while Marian worked on her watercolor painting. But after little more than an hour her cousin was awake and ready to talk.

"I have been thinking, Marian," she began, while considering which gown she would wear that evening, "that I should very much like an offer from Lord Sidley."

Marian drew a sharp breath and dabbed at the unintentional bloom of paint before her. "You are certain, Katie?"

"About the offer, indeed. It is so important, you see, that everyone know I receive it."

"If you accept him, 'twill be supposed."

"But I've no intention of accepting him."

Marian turned to her impatiently. "What are you on about, Katie?"

"Just that I—I like Lord Sidley. I truly do, Marian. But he is so very *old*. Almost twenty-nine! And I think—in fact, I *know*—I should most definitely like another season, or even two, before I become Lady Sidley."

"He does not have that time, Cousin."

"Oh, I know. Even if I might have many seasons as Lady Sidley, I should be in mourning two years. And unable to dance! I should abhor it above all things. But he does not seem so terribly ill, does he, Marian? Just a bit slow. Although there is something in his manner—something that reminds me of Papa—that I find I cannot quite like."

Marian silently credited Katie with more insight than she had displayed to date. Sidley did treat Katie as though she were less a partner than a charge.

"Then why should you wish an offer, Katie? Because it is a matter of pride?"

Katie was nodding vigorously. "Too many know that I've—that I've claimed to want one. I cannot turn back now!"

"But what of Lord Sidley's pride, you goose? Do you think he will enjoy such a refusal?"

"I think he will offer for someone else straightaway," she said practically. "I expect Becca Harvey would have him."

You are wrong there, Marian thought silently. *Delia shall have him.*

"Anyway," Katie continued, "I might need your help tonight, to bring him up to scratch."

"And how shall I do that, pray?"

"When you talk with him, you must remind him that other gentlemen have been most attentive to me in town."

"He knows that already, Katie. You are wildly popular. But Lord Sidley will not compete."

"Oh, yes he will," she claimed. "All gentlemen do."

Marian sighed. "If I speak with him, I will mention it. But why should he listen to me?"

"He seems to admire you—as an artist. He always has something to say to you. This afternoon he was asking me about your home in Brinford. And he's asked several times about William, whom I've only met the once, and that long ago, when I was fifteen. Lord Sidley has little to say to me unless it concerns you."

"He finds me a curiosity, Katie. An oddity, nothing more. He searches for reasons to tease me."

"He teases you as well? Then I shan't find it so vexing."

When they at last went downstairs, music already flooded the common rooms. There were just enough couples among Aldersham's guests to insure that all who wished to stand up to dance could do so, however small the set. When Marian came to dance with Edgar, she queried him about his fascination with Rebecca Harvey.

"Good Lord, Marian, you sound as frosty as Mother! Becca is absolutely wonderful! You should have seen her ride today—she cleared a six-foot hedge on the way home as though it were no more than a line of pebbles! And she was on that nervy gray hunter of Sidley's too! Ripping rider!"

"Yes, but Edgar, are you serious? What do you know of her character? Are you intending to speak to her father, to make her—"

"I might, Marian. I very well might. And if I do,

then you and Mother and Katie shall simply have to accept her!"

"If she accepts you."

"I'm almost certain she would," he said. "If Benjamin, who hasn't a single worthy impulse, would leave off pestering her! He shouldn't think Becca entertains any charity toward him at all, with him just the least of Derwin's brood—"

"She has given you reason to hope, then, Cousin?"

"More than hope, Marian! The way she smiles at me—as though we share some secret of our own . . ."

As his raptures continued, Marian ceased to comment. Her gaze slid to Sidley, who danced farther down the set with Edith. Apparently he was having no difficulty executing the steps. She watched him turn. And his own gaze caught her watching him.

At once she focused intently on Lord Vaughn, who passed her in the line. Lord Benjamin had told them of Vaughn's history with Jenny Lanning, now Mrs. Knox. Marian found herself thinking that Vaughn also cared for someone beyond reach. She knew her consideration held compassion. She felt herself coloring at the thought, but she doubted the viscount read her expression correctly. He was a most grave-looking gentleman.

They did not dance long. Edith and Lady Adeline left the floor, shrinking the set. Lord Sidley and the Harveys excused themselves from the subsequent lively gigue, which was the last dance preceding a late supper. In the dining room, Marian was once more assigned to the center of the table, across from Clara Poole. Marian was thoroughly ashamed of herself and of her betraying, ambitious heart; for, however much she might wish to think of him, she could not seem to summon William. And though Sidley was too readily in her thoughts, she refused to contemplate *him.* She would not look toward her host at the head of the table and concentrated instead on moving her untouched supper about her plate.

Her host's choice of bride had to be near at hand. She told herself she was prepared. Yet when the group retired for the night, no announcement had been made, and Marian was left to confront a final morning of work on Lord Sidley's portrait.

Sidley had debated with himself for much of the night—whether to speak to her or not. He'd determined that as either course bore with it a certain measure of risk, he might as soon opt for the happier.

And so he told Vaughn as they rode the next morning. "I must choose, Vaughn. Why should I not choose what gives me pleasure?"

"Miss Ware is affianced."

"But she is not yet *married.* I have your example before me, my friend. How should I feel were she to marry Lieutenant Reeves? I should forever regret not having spoken."

"You anticipate, then, that she might break her engagement?"

Sidley drew his horse to a halt and measured Vaughn's expression. "She is not indifferent to me."

"Possibly not. But she is honor-bound; she must still feel committed. She is like to think you forward."

"Better that than that we should both be too slavish to propriety—and miserable as well."

"You assume much, Lee. From what I perceive of Miss Ware, she has not dared to think of you in that way. You have been courting her cousin. Would you expect her to be overjoyed by your disclosure? Think of her concerns for her family. And do not forget—you have not apprised her or the Formsbys of your true state of health."

"I shall do so this morning. My perceived ill health shall no longer prove an obstacle."

"No, but your *health* might."

"My cryptic friend, just what do you mean?"

"What I have told you before. That she will not appreciate having been taken for a fool."

"I never sought to dupe her. Nor have I implied that my days are numbered."

"The powder . . . ?"

"Has been entirely dispensed with. Granted, Vaughn, 'tis a delicate matter. But she must be happier to know me living than dying."

"She might still choose not to live *with* you."

"I shall risk that."

Vaughn looked down as he patted his horse's neck. "I have rarely questioned your wisdom, Sidley. And heaven knows we have seen a good deal together. But if

I were a betting man, I would lay you odds you will be surprised."

"She cannot be in ignorance of my sentiments."

Vaughn's eyebrows rose. "She may be aware of your attentions but still fail to comprehend your aim. *I* do not comprehend your aim. You are not being entirely rational, Lee. And your actions have spoken louder than whatever you might wish to say to her. Regardless of her own sentiments or wishes, she knows you have been wooing three other women. I remind you, 'twas not Miss Ware you escorted about the lake yesterday."

"The circuits were to please my aunt."

"And as for that, do you think Lady Adeline will approve this choice?"

"She likes Miss Ware. And the girl is still a Satterthwaite."

"But she is not at your level. She has neither title nor, as I hear it, much of a portion. Her standing is not nearly as elevated as her cousin's, or even Miss Tinckney-Dwight's. And she hasn't the treasures of the Harveys."

"She has much more of value. And she thinks for herself."

"Commendable, I'm sure. But she cannot *act* entirely for herself. Lee, you forget she is a woman."

Sidley smiled. "I assure you, I do not forget it."

"You forget its restrictions. I caution you—"

"I care for the girl, Arthur."

Vaughn sighed. "If you truly care for her, she deserves better from you. You must not speak."

"Must not? Then you must tell me how I should manage. For I suspect you would know better than most." For his sharpness, he had the dubious satisfaction of silencing Vaughn. "My friend," he said quickly, "I am sorry. I'm not used to such speeches from you; no doubt I deserve it. But I feel I must take the chance."

"It is not a gamble in your favor, Sidley. You have forgotten yourself in your pretense." And with that warning, Vaughn continued disconsolately by his side to the edge of the stable yard.

There, just as they reined in, Sidley noticed that Marian Ware stepped into the open doorway at the west wing of the house. She wore her painting smock, which proved she had already been at work. He smiled even as he managed a careful dismount.

"Now is as good a time as any," he muttered to Vaughn, who nodded abruptly and obligingly led the horses off to be stabled. But Sidley's assurance diminished the closer he got to the house. For however charming Marian Ware looked in her serviceable smock, however appealingly fresh her cheeks and bright her hair in the early-morning light, the expression on her face was lethal.

He halted abruptly.

She remained several steps above him and looked down. The lift of her chin was contemptuous. "I saw you from the library," she said, "as you crossed the front drive." She pressed her palms together, as though she would contain herself. "You look very fit this morning, my lord. In fact, you do not look ill at all."

"Miss Ware—"

"I have been blind," she rushed on. "Not to see, not to know, that there is nothing whatever the matter with you! Yet here I have been *painting* you and not—not *seeing* you!"

Even as she seethed, she looked lovely.

"Miss Ware—" he tried again.

"I suppose I must be monstrously susceptible." Her sharply drawn breath was audible. "To have believed it—all the talk, all the gossip that you and your callous friends have put about. I still cannot credit you with acting so contemptibly, given your family, and Lord Vaughn as well, and Lord Benjamin. 'Tis unconscionable!"

"Miss Ware, I would—"

"How cynical you must be," she charged, "to engage in such a hoax, when here I thought you merely high-spirited! Whatever could have put it into your head? That all of this"—she gestured vaguely—"should be nothing but a game to you, some insufferable joke, a moment's caprice, when there are those who sincerely wished you—" She stopped and fixed him with a magnificently dampening stare.

"Clara Poole termed you 'playful' yesterday, my lord, and she must know, because she is your friend of long-standing. You have not dared deceive her. But *I* would call you devious. Devious and cruel! All these manipulations—to what purpose? More attention, I suppose, for one of your outrageous conceit. Or perhaps you laugh at those who truly have been injured, and you make a mockery of their troubles and commitment, to prove life itself a jest? Your poor aunt! What she must be feeling! And all so you might gallivant unchecked about town! That you should be so irresponsible! Oh, you *are* 'useless'! Just as he said! I shall never forgive you. I shall never, ever forgive you!"

"Oh, come now," he said, attempting a step toward her. "Miss Marian—"

But she moved back. "I cannot stop you from courting Katie." Her voice was sharper, harder. "I can only influence how she thinks of you. My aunt and Edgar will aid me in leaving today, Lord Sidley, when I request it. They will not question me. They trust me, as they should no longer trust *you*. You may explain yourself to them in your own way. I will grant you that one small courtesy, here—in your home. But if you do not tell them soon, I promise you that *I* shall. And I will leave within the hour."

"Miss Marian, you must listen!" He was becoming distractedly aware of a horrific din from the stables, and from somewhere at the back of the house a woman was shrieking, shrieking to the uttermost at seven o'clock in the morning. He wished only to concentrate on Marian Ware, yet he had to force himself to ignore the ungodly noise. "Please, listen—"

"No doubt you have some ready explanation," she interrupted. Her cheeks were very pink. The stream of charges had come from her almost breathlessly. "No doubt you have practiced it, and possibly you even believe it sound. But it cannot be. You have demonstrated the most insufferable arrogance! That you, who have so much, should have stooped . . . oh, it is despicable, sir! Your behavior has been vile. And I must regret my own. I am ashamed. I'm appalled that I thought you—"

The shrieking had become unbearable. Sidley's jaw set grimly.

"I wish never to see you again," she said abruptly, and wheeled from him.

He started up the steps after her, only to be brought up short.

"Sidley!" Vaughn had a hold of his arm. "Becca Harvey's decamped. Before dawn this morning. Her father thinks she's off to Gretna Green."

"Benny?" Sidley grated impatiently, watching Marian Ware's retreating back.

"No, thank God. Linton Mopes, that fool curricle racer from town."

"Mopes! She will regret it. And her parents?"

"Her mother is in hysterics. You must come. Harvey intends to set out after them at once."

Sidley looked in frustration down the hallway. Marian Ware had vanished. And he could not pursue her. Not now. His obligation was to the Harveys, whose foolish daughter had had the poor judgment to flee an earl's house party, and before breakfast.

"Fast horses," he muttered to Vaughn, turning with him to stride toward the stables. He felt ill, as he had not felt ill in weeks. "'Twas Miss Harvey's future, was it not?" And he thought his own looked more than bleak.

Chapter Nine

What Marian recalled of their confrontation was her desire to hurt him. Yet the pain had been her own, and it had lingered—beyond any remembrance of what she had said and even past another week in town.

Rebecca Harvey's elopement had given Marian every excuse to urge a precipitous departure from Aldersham and Kent. Edgar had been equally eager to leave the scene, his pride in eclipse after Becca's perceived betrayal. He had accompanied Marian and Katie in returning early to London, leaving Lady Formsby to counsel her friend Lady Adeline as best she might and for as many days as she felt necessary.

Their carriage trip back had been made at a rapid pace and all in a day. Yet even at that spanking speed, Mr. Harvey and Lord Sidley had preceded them to town, where Becca Harvey's marriage to Mr. Mopes by special license had instantly been all the talk. The hasty London wedding had only partly allayed the Harveys' fears. For Linton Mopes was widely deemed a poor bargain, an acknowledged fortune hunter who had succeeded, at last, in obtaining a prize.

The marriage had placed Mrs. Harvey at the core of the very gossip she relished, but Marian's sympathies were still with her and her shocked husband, who had wished much better for their adored only child. Though she had grown keenly aware of the vagaries of attraction, Marian still could not understand Becca's choice. One might, she supposed, be ready to wed another on the basis of several weeks' acquaintance. But surely a person of sense did not break every other commitment to family, friends, and society?

I am become narrow-minded, she thought to herself, and she concentrated on her painting of Edith's garden. She had been excused from class that day, as the rest were to draw from a male model. Marian had resigned herself to the exclusion, for Edith had finally returned from Aldersham very late the night before. As Marian had not seen Edith in almost a week, she was curious to hear if Lord Sidley had confessed his ruse to Lady Adeline—and if the Tinckney-Dwights had been similarly enlightened.

She wished as well to discuss William. She knew that ending her engagement would prompt a desire for an explanation; the change also burdened her with seeking an extension of her stay with the Formsby family. She anticipated that she must return to Brinford at some point, since she could not spend the rest of her days with her cousins. But perhaps, and most contrarily, for what little time she remained in town, she might at least occasionally glimpse Lord Sidley . . .

"Do come inside now, Marian. The sun is too high," Edith called. She stood shading her eyes at the open door to the terrace.

Marian, shielded by a slouchy, soft-brimmed country hat, smiled at her. "I shall come directly," she promised. She quickly cleaned her brushes. Leaving her easel at its spot in the garden, she collected her canvas and the rest of her supplies.

In the shadows just inside the door to the drawing room, Lord Sidley stood watching her as she entered.

"Allow me, Miss Ware," he said pleasantly, reaching to take the paint box from her hand. Though he managed to collect part of her burden, Marian pulled back sharply.

"I ran into Sidley at Jackson's this morning and asked him by," Edgar told her loftily.

Marian scarcely heard him, though she was aware that several other people stood within the drawing room— Katie and Edith and Lord Benjamin. Sidley's face was still in shadow, or else her eyes had not adjusted from the brightness out-of-doors. Impatiently she swept her practical, unfashionable hat from her head, immediately regretting her action when he smiled at her.

"Where should you like these, Miss Ware?" he asked.

She did not answer him but walked with her canvas across the room and out into the hall. She propped her painting against the wall at the foot of the stairs, then reached to take her supplies from him.

"Your utter gall . . ." she began under her breath.

"I was invited," he countered calmly. "And I must speak with you."

She dared then to meet his eyes. In the past she would have gauged his look sincere; she would have found the only problem to be with the rapid beat of her heart. But now she did not trust him.

She marched back into the drawing room. Accepting a glass of lemonade from Edith, she settled herself on an exceedingly narrow settee. That Sidley chose to sit next to her, though there really wasn't room, set her teeth on edge.

"This is cozy," he remarked softly. "Perhaps you have already forgiven me?"

His smile infuriated her. She shifted as far away from him as possible, though her skirts still brushed his boot.

"Lord Sidley has brought us some surprising news, Marian!" Katie said. "Miss Tinckney-Dwight has accepted a proposal of marriage from Mr. Poole." Katie was beaming.

Marian had no doubt as to why. With both Becca and Delia removed from contention for Sidley's favors, Katie must anticipate an offer at any moment. Marian could not help but look to Sidley.

" 'Twas indeed a surprise, Miss Ware," he conceded. "Even last week I had thought Dicky's interest fixed on *you*."

"Mr. Poole is a gentleman," she countered sharply. "He knew me to be engaged."

The small smile in answer to that incensed her.

"Sir Philip seems as happy about the match as Dicky and Miss Delia," he said. "After all, their temperaments are well suited. And as neither needs to marry, one can assume them more than content."

"You are quite the matchmaker, my lord," Marian said shortly.

"D'you think so? My recent house party will certainly be renowned."

"You must not feel you are to blame, Lord Sidley," Edith said. "Your aunt told me she had made up the guest list."

"Just so, ma'am." Sidley nodded to her. "Lady Adeline confesses to playing Cupid. I certainly had no such intention."

"Far from it!" Lord Benjamin offered. "If anything—"

"You must tell us, Benny, of your decision," Sidley prompted quickly. "Lord Benjamin is joining the 10th Regiment of Dragoons—the Hussars."

"Are you?" Edgar asked, with more interest and courtesy than he had ever shown Lord Benjamin during their feud over Becca Harvey.

"It should put me out of the petticoat line for some

time, I imagine, Formsby," Benny conceded with a laugh.

And while the purchase of a commission was the center of discussion, Sidley rose to his feet.

"I hope you do not mind, Lady Formsby, Lady Katherine—I should like a word with Miss Ware regarding the completion of her portrait. There are some tedious artistic details to be gone over. May we excuse ourselves for a few minutes?" He was indicating the terrace. Clutching her glass of lemonade, Marian glanced at her aunt in alarm. But Edith looked complaisant. And Katie, assured in her impending triumph, simply smiled benignly.

Marian rose stiffly. Placing her drink aside, she preceded Sidley out the door. The terrace provided little enough privacy, yet he seemed determined to make the most of any available distance. He walked to the stone balusters and rail along its farthest edge and stood with his back to the drawing-room door.

"I know you are still very angry, Miss Ware," he said calmly. "And I know you believe yourself angry with cause. But I should like you to listen to me." He looked at the garden below as he spoke. "I ask for your fairness. If nothing else you owe it to your cousins, whose house this is, and who are my hosts." His brief glance at her was a challenge. Marian looked quickly back over her shoulder toward the drawing room's dim interior, but Sidley soon commanded her attention.

"First, I must set your mind at ease. I have no intention of offering for Lady Katherine. She may believe she wants an offer from me—in certain quarters an offer may be expected. I know it is the dearest wish of my aunt. Perhaps it is Lady Formsby's as well—I do not know. But much as I esteem your cousin, I also know we should not suit. And it is abundantly clear that Lady Katherine's heart is not at risk. I shall endeavor to prove this to her in the kindest way possible over the coming week. I would never dishonor her; you need not defend her from my dreaded 'manipulations.' " When she would have spoken, the mere lift of his eyebrows stopped her.

"Second, of all of which you accused me last week, Miss Ware, you charged me perhaps most profoundly with deceiving my aunt. Let me assure you that Lady Adeline has always known of the precise state of my health, even when I myself was conscious of nothing." His blue gaze briefly flashed at her. " 'Tis true I ceased to counter the widespread speculations regarding my illness. Exaggerations of the nature of my indisposition were rife, Miss Ware. You, who have little knowledge of the *ton*'s obsessions, may not fully appreciate how tenacious false rumors become. For many weeks I was unable even to attempt to deny them, and then once I *was* able, my efforts proved not only ineffective but strangely counter to my purpose. At times I thought many wished me dead for the sheer entertainment of it. After some weeks I elected to let the situation work to my advantage. You will consider such a decision beneath me." He turned briefly again to look at her but quickly turned back. "I can only plead that everyone is due a holiday at some time. I determined to take mine, *gratis,* when it seemed unlikely to hurt anyone. That it has caused you distress is a rebuke to me. I apologize for it."

He sighed. "Perhaps, had you been wiser in the ways of the *ton,* you would not have invested me with such lofty qualities. You are a truthful person, a person of integrity. You accuse me of lying to you and to others. I say only that I did not pose with any intention of harm. Did I gain sympathy and attention I would not otherwise have had? Perhaps. But the sheer weight of speculation had already brought me such; I did not seek it. And in your case"—again he looked at her—"in your case, Miss Ware, I found I sought your company and knew of no gentlemanly way to obtain it."

Marian was having difficulty keeping her gaze from his face. He was freshly shaven, free of powder. He still looked pale without it, but he also looked superb. She had always thought he looked so.

"You should not have sought my company," she managed.

"That I could not control." He smiled. As they heard Katie's laughter from the room behind them, he propped himself against the stone rail and faced Marian. "I am no longer a youngster, Miss Ware. I told you at Aldersham how I must wed shortly. And now, having failed with my most likely prospects, I must begin anew."

She tilted her chin. "That cannot be such a trial for you, my lord."

"Perhaps you yourself are so satisfactorily settled that you cannot summon the least bit of sympathy." His gaze held hers for a moment. Then he smiled. "I do not mean to boast, when I tell you that I am apparently considered a frighteningly eligible *parti*. If you cannot sympathize, perhaps you might still spare some understanding? 'Twas the thought of freeing myself from the weight of so much expectation that furthered my ruse. You shall no doubt hear, now that I am returned to the living, how briefly my bachelor existence endures."

"It is a shame that you lost Miss Tinckney-Dwight. You seemed very—congenial."

Again his fine eyebrows rose. "You are most presumptuous, Miss Ware. Miss Delia has chosen the better man. I believe she found me too serious, much too somber. My mind was often elsewhere."

She felt his attention to her face. She focused on the garden, which she had observed closely on a regular basis. She had painted it often; the thought prompted her question.

"What of your—what of your portrait, Lord Sidley? Did you truly wish to discuss it?" She thought he sighed.

"I should like you to finish it, if you can force yourself to do so. My aunt likes it exceedingly. And I believe it is turning out well enough."

Well enough? She eyed him. "Where is it?" she asked.

"I had it brought to town. I might send it on to you here

if you are so inclined. And if you feel you might work on it away from Aldersham. I had hoped to complete the project this season."

"I needn't work at Aldersham. But I might . . . need you, my lord—"

"Why, Miss Ware! How charming."

"Very briefly," she finished, with an impatient gesture of one hand. "My aunt should not mind if I work here just once in the drawing room."

"I shall be on my best behavior."

"Was there anything else, Lord Sidley?" She could tell he did not much care for her clipped tone, but she was conscious of the time they had spent in private conversation. Such time alone was the last thing she had wanted, and her anxiety mounted.

"Only that Miss Poole will be visiting with us when my aunt returns to town. Clara asked to be remembered to you and wondered if she might call on you."

"But, of course! I would be delighted. I enjoy her company."

"This is, naturally, dependent on your own schedule. When does Lieutenant Reeves arrive?"

The question seemed abrupt. She did not think of William's arrival; she had quite pointedly not thought of it.

"Within the week, I believe. Though he may not come here to me in town. I expect he intends to travel on to Brinford, where I shall . . . I shall join him."

"Then we must take care not to waste your limited time." He straightened and turned to her. "You have found my behavior wanting on more than one occasion. I believe I have also failed to offer you proper felicitations on your betrothal. I hope you will forgive me for the oversight. 'Twas yet more evidence of what you rightly termed my 'outrageous conceit.' " His smile was rueful. "I do wish you happy."

"Thank you, my lord." She felt wretched. She struggled to find a distraction. "Where is Lord Vaughn?"

"Vaughn stopped at his estate in Surrey. The place required his attention. But he will be back shortly."

"I thought him your shadow," she said, and tried to force a smile.

"Perhaps I am his." At her silence he added, "We are great friends. Which reminds me. There is one other matter that has concerned me. I believe I might be of aid—"

"Lord Sidley?" Katie called. She pouted as she stood in the doorway. "Lord Benjamin has told us you have had nothing whatever to eat today! Will you not take some refreshment?"

"We come at once, my lady," he said. He placed his gloved hand lightly beneath Marian's elbow to escort her the short distance back across the flagstone; Marian felt his clasp every step of the way.

He stayed only a few minutes longer, to sample a biscuit Katherine pressed upon him and to commend Edgar's purchase of a dappled gray saddle horse. And when he and Lord Benjamin departed, Marian was left more restive than ever.

Lord Sidley had made a miraculous recovery. No fewer than three respected physicians, none of whom had examined his lordship, commented publicly on the extraordinary nature of the case. Every aspect of Lord Sidley's routine—his diet, his exercise, his habits—was scrutinized minutely for keys to his reversal. The slavish, pitying attention that had followed his projected doom now seemed equally enthralled with his inexplicable improvement.

Such an energetic round of dances, dinners, and romps had heralded Sidley's return to the living that he began during the week to feel himself in some danger of a relapse. So it was that before accompanying his aunt to the theater one fine June evening, he sat discussing his affairs with Vaughn.

"I have arranged to visit the Formsbys," Sidley said, "to let Miss Ware finish up my portrait. You would be proud of me, my friend, for I have not seen Miss Ware these past three days. I am leaving her to her sailor."

Vaughn eyed him. "Shall I commend you for what should not have taken effort?" he asked.

"Yes, devil it! Because it did take effort! And more, besides. I have not been able to avoid Lady Katherine, who still flings herself about, enjoying the last faint flutters of the season. The girl will drive me into an early grave."

"An irony there, certainly. But I hear you have introduced her to young Lord Carroll. There is some speculation that she is taken with the fellow."

"A boyish, empty-headed Adonis! Yet even as a mere baron, he must trump a lame and elderly earl. I believe she is enchanted with his dancing and driving skills, as well as his golden curls. I have tried hard to withhold my distaste for Carroll, Vaughn, given that 'twas he and Mopes who came closest to actually killing me with their mad curricle race." He grimaced. "I'm reminded that whilst we toured Iberia, these young blades were spending their families' fortunes on gaming and horses. Still, I suppose I must grant that they gained a certain prowess."

"You are not yet so aged, Sidley, that you could not best them at the ribbons."

"I've no wish to. Let them saddle themselves with the Becca Harveys and Lady Katherines. I've no taste for gambling with life when I needn't."

"Which leaves you with just whom for a countess, my friend? You still mean to satisfy your aunt?"

Sidley gazed thoughtfully at his brandy. "I think I must discuss with Lady Adeline the possibility of approaching a widow, or someone distinctly on the shelf. I am in the mood to be treated with gratitude, as a bit of a savior. 'Twould be balm to the wounds to have someone appreciate my attentions. These young diamonds have no sense of what is due me."

Vaughn laughed. "Meek gratitude would satisfy you

all of ten minutes, Sidley. You do not understand your-self."

"That is not the case. I simply cannot have what I wish."

Vaughn looked contemplatively up at the painting over the mantel. The Constable, purchased by Sidley's father just before his younger son's departure for the war, depicted a simple country scene—little more than an English river, an English cottage, and several sturdy English oaks. Yet Sidley knew it so intimately that he had been able to describe it in detail, and frequently, to Vaughn as they traversed the Peninsula.

"I heard that the lieutenant's ship, the *Perseus,* docked at Portsmouth yesterday," Vaughn said.

"Did it?" Sidley checked the first wild leap of his blood—the very desire to prove himself, to fight and to win, that made such fools of the youngsters. "Then to-morrow is not soon enough to have my portrait finished. Miss Ware shall not be Miss Ware much longer."

"You must grant that hers is a practical decision, Sid-ley. Sensible young women do not toss aside solid prospects to be favored for a few weeks by their betters."

Sidley scowled. "You think me so lacking in honor?"

"I think you are not yourself. I think you are not think-ing."

Again Sidley idly swirled the untouched brandy in his glass. "Miss Ware wishes to paint Jenny Knox," he said abruptly, and he watched Vaughn blanch. "Yes, I thought so," he added. "This is not a matter of thinking, Vaughn, but of feeling. All of us must, apparently, play our pre-scribed parts. But I cannot deceive myself that the outcomes are in any regard optimal. Decidedly not." Placing the snifter to the side, he rose to his feet. "Some days ago she sent me a watercolor sketch. Though she claims she drew it up as a preliminary, I suspect she must have worked on it as something quite apart." He walked to a bureau and, opening an upper drawer, carefully re-moved a tissue-wrapped sheet of thick paper. Uncover-ing it, he held it up for Vaughn's inspection.

Vaughn regarded it for a long moment, then said frankly, "You told me she painted with the best. I affirm it."

Sidley's smile was humorless. "'Twas done with some affection, would you not say so, Vaughn?"

"I imagine she paints what she feels, which lends the piece its power. But you must still interpret. And what has changed? Even if she does return your sentiments, you would have her break her promise to a man who has been at sea these past two years?"

"Worse things have happened," Sidley said intently. "What must an engagement be, after all? 'Tis meant to be short of a marriage."

"But not, perhaps, as flexible as you would wish it. We've discussed this before."

Sidley sighed. "You do know, Vaughn, that this is in-supportable."

"But you shall bear it."

"Yes," he said with resignation. And having to some

degree at last reached that state of acceptance, and hearing Lady Adeline and Miss Poole in the hall, the two men departed in considerable melancholy for the evening's effort at entertainment.

With some uneasiness Marian set up her easel in one of the Formsbys' drawing rooms. The afternoon was bright, but her spirits were dim. She suspected this would be the last time she would paint Lord Sidley, and she greeted the prospect with both expectation and sadness. Forwarding the watercolor portrait to him had been as close as she dared come to confessing her feelings, but she had heard nothing from him in response, which she admitted to herself was all for the best. Perhaps he had concluded only that she wished to finish with all things Sidley; perhaps what had seemed so obvious to her had not conveyed clearly to him. Indeed, she had been of two minds whether to part with the token at all. The watercolor had not been what she determined he wanted in a formal portrait—she had sketched him quickly, standing in the library at Aldersham and looking rather soberly out at the garden. She had drawn him that first day, when he had worn his black coat and she debated how best to pose him. But she had captured some part of him in that portrait, something fresh and intimate, that had so far eluded her in the larger oil. If she could identify the difference today, she knew her work would be all the better for it.

"Lord Sidley, miss," Jenks announced, with Sidley at his heels.

"My lord."

"Miss Ware."

Two footmen guarded the open door to the drawing room. Marian noted them absently as she looked to Sidley. She thought he looked less than pleased to be present.

"My aunt and Lady Katherine should be back shortly, my lord. They have gone shopping. I hope you do not mind if we begin?"

"I am at your command."

She had him take a seat with the light from the terrace window to the side. It was afternoon light and not as clear here in the city as it had been in Kent. But Marian's effort today was to check Sidley's features and to unify the values of his hair, complexion, and coat. For the rest, she still remembered Aldersham. She could recall the feel of a morning there from memory.

"The town is full of news of your recovery, my lord," she said.

"That is only a slight exaggeration, Miss Ware, as the visits of the Russian tsar and king of Prussia have drawn some middling attention for weeks. As has word of the abdication of a former emperor—what the devil was his name? Ah, I see that you smile about it now. Does that mean you have forgiven me?"

"It should not matter what I think, my—"

"But it does."

"Then yes," she said, purposely hiding behind the canvas. "I have forgiven you."

"I am most grateful for that. And grateful as well for the watercolor, which is splendid. With your permission I shall have it framed."

"The sketch is yours to do with as you please. I fear you may be happier with it than with this oil. For I cannot get it right . . ."

"I have no objection to continuing our sessions. But I forget—you are shortly to leave us. I understand that Lieutenant Reeves's ship has docked at Portsmouth."

Then you know more than I, Marian thought silently. She fought the slight tremor in her hand and kept painting.

"I must thank you, my lord, for directing Lord Carroll to Katie. No, do not shake your head. I know that you did so. I believe she goes driving with Carroll in the park later this afternoon. You have set my mind at ease."

"You may not thank me should she develop a *tendre* for Carroll, though he is better than many."

"Katie is, thankfully, not ready to give her heart. And as she is in the enviable position of not needing to marry, she has chosen to enjoy every aspect of the season."

"I am well aware of *that.* I am exhausted."

Marian laughed. She tried to concentrate on the painting before her. But she had just then realized why she faced a difficulty with the oil that she had not with the watercolor sketch. She had painted the earlier piece knowing that she found Lord Sidley attractive, that she liked him, and that she regretted his ill health and imminent loss. She had painted with feeling, but she had not recognized just how deep her feelings ran.

She struggled to focus. Having asked him here, she could not very well abandon the session.

"You have a delightful laugh," Sidley said, drawing her attention to his eyes. She believed he must read her thoughts on her face. "Although I cannot claim it is reassuring to have the artist laugh while recording one's likeness."

She smiled. "Miss Poole did not accompany you today? I expected she might."

"Clara also shops this afternoon, with my aunt, for a wedding gift for Dicky. Apparently such selections require considerable application. Perhaps you will be as attentive to your own brother's nuptials."

In all truth Marian had given little thought to Michael's wedding, which he planned for November. November seemed so very far in the future.

"I shall most probably offer to paint his bride, my lord."

"I had forgotten that you will always be capable of offering the most rewarding gift possible."

"You tease me, Lord Sidley. It is, for me, also the least expensive."

"I'm convinced that will not long be the case. I assume you will have submissions prepared for next summer's Royal Academy exhibition?"

"I have some paintings and drawings that might be

acceptable, and I will apply myself to more. But as you know, the exhibition is juried. I must pass muster."

" 'Tis competitive, certainly, but you will have no difficulty. I believe the standard is 'distinguished merit.' "

"I appreciate your confidence, my lord."

"I am no less confident than you are, Miss Ware, to have embarked on this course at all. I believe you deserve to succeed. To that end, I wish you would permit me to open some doors for you."

Marian's brush hand wavered. "How do you mean?" she asked.

"I should like to introduce you to Mr. Angerstein, who owns a large number of masterpieces. He shows his collection at his home in Pall Mall. And there are others of my acquaintance who further the arts—John Varley, who still teaches, and whose watercolors I am certain you know, and Dr. Monro, who supported Turner. Perhaps old Sir George Beaumont might even be prevailed upon—"

"Why should you do this, Lord Sidley?"

"Why should I not? As I've mentioned, 'tis within my power. And these gentlemen might interest you, and aid you."

" 'Tis not necessary for you to make—to compensate—for anything. You have already done more than enough with this commission. I would not ask you—"

"You are due the opportunities because of your ability. I ask nothing of you in return. Except, perhaps, that you think well of me."

"I needn't take such advantage. I do think well of you."

"How well?"

She stopped painting and met his gaze. The intensity of his made her breath catch. *He knows,* she thought. *He understood the watercolor.* Even as she thought it, she wished she might capture the openness of his gaze on the canvas. But first she had to answer it.

"My lord—"

"Do not 'my lord' me, Marian."

Her heart faltered, even as footsteps crossed the hall. She thought Edith and Katie had returned.

But at the doorway the butler announced, "Lieutenant Reeves to see you, miss."

Chapter Ten

William was tanned and healthy. He was smiling broadly. Marian could not help but view him with relief; for two years she had feared for his safety. And the waiting—the waiting had seemed endless. But as she carefully laid her brush aside and crossed quickly to the doorway, she sensed Sidley's gaze upon her. And, despite the smile, William looked as ill at ease as she felt.

In the second's hesitation before she could reach to kiss his cheek, William grasped her hand and smartly saluted it.

"Hello, old girl," he said. "You look just—just as ever."

"William!" she breathed, "I did not expect you. Not here in town."

"No, of course not. Didn't mean to surprise you, but Michael thought I should come on to you first thing."

"Michael! But where is *he*?"

"In Brinford. Had a letter from him, I mean."

Marian stared at him. Something was wrong. But William's gaze had slid to Sidley.

"My—Lord Sidley," she said, turning to him. "May I present Lieutenant William Reeves?"

Sidley had risen to his feet. He bowed, as did William.

"How d'you do, Lieutenant?" Sidley was smiling. "I have heard much of you."

"You have? I can't imagine—"

"Your fiancée has been most complimentary."

To Marian's surprise, William blushed a bright red.

"Too . . . too kind. Thank you, my lord." He cleared his throat. "Marian paints you?"

Sidley gestured to the canvas. When William crossed the room, Sidley joined him in appraising the work.

"Good of you to let Marian practice on you, my lord."

"The honor is mine." He paused. "Are you not impressed with the result, Lieutenant?"

"It does look very much like you, my lord. That is always most important. You must have preferred, though, to be painted in your regimentals? I wonder Marian did not think of it."

"Miss Ware did think of it, Lieutenant. But it was not my preference."

"Well . . . He looked uncomfortable and straightened his shoulders. "It should have been mine."

Sidley's smile did not reach his eyes. "Quite." He was watching William's face. "I do not wonder at it."

Marian took some umbrage at his tone, which she deemed critical. She knew that Sidley observed her—worse, that he observed her with William. He could not have failed to note the constraint between them.

"I must congratulate you, Lieutenant, on securing Miss Ware's affections."

"Well, as to that, she is . . . she is something. . . ."

"Something, yes." Sidley's gaze fell lazily upon her, in such a manner that Marian grew warm. "I know you must have much to impart to each other," he said, moving toward the door, and Marian, conscious of a curious reluctance to let him leave, followed him. She should not have desired Lord Sidley's help with her fiancé. The thought was ludicrous.

Sidley paused at the entry to the hall and turned to her. "We never quite finish, do we?" he asked softly. Taking the same bare hand William had just saluted, he raised it to his lips and placed a kiss upon the selfsame spot. But there was nothing at all similar in its effect. His gaze assessed her as he donned his hat and gathered his gloves and cane. "You look lovely, Miss Ware—just as ever," he said, pointedly amending William's words. Then he moved into the hall and left her.

"Well!" William said as she returned to him.

The back of her hand felt precious.

"You are keeping high company these days, Marian. Sidley! And painting him! What is he paying you?"

"I do not know." She gestured airily and stared very

hard for a second out the window into the garden. "He promises something."

"Should have settled with him first. These nobs sometimes take what they can—"

"Lord Sidley wouldn't."

William's eyebrows rose. "He favors one leg," he remarked. "Just the slightest bit. He was injured at Toulouse, wasn't he?"

"Orthez. I believe it was Orthez. It is all much more than you wish to know, William. Let us not talk of Lord Sidley just now. Here you are returned and looking very well! But how could you have had a letter from Michael? Did your ship not just arrive?"

Again he blushed. "He knew we were due about now and sent the note to await me. You see, I'd—I'd written him from Gibraltar."

"You wrote me as well, but I'm still surprised to see you here in town. I thought you meant to go on to Brinford and that I would join you there."

"That *was* the plan. But, well, Michael thought I should—said it would be best if I came directly to you here. Naturally I was most eager to see you." But his gaze was roaming the room, as though he were far from eager to see her. In fact, he appeared to be looking everywhere but at her. The smart uniform served only to emphasize his unease. Marian wondered if Sidley had seen that in him. Again she sensed something was wrong.

"What is it, William?" she asked abruptly. "Has something happened to Michael?"

"Michael? Oh, no, not at all." At last his gaze returned to her. "This is entirely—well, Marian, we have known each other a very long time. I can certainly tell *you* that . . . that I have married!"

"Married?"

A grin was breaking across his face. The grin did not seem to suit what he had said.

"You mean, you have married someone else?"

"Yes. In Gibraltar. Before we sailed. My Rose is— Oh, Marian! You must understand! Had I not wed her *then,* 'twould have been another six months, and that would have been much too long to wait! We—we love each other, Marian. I could not have asked her to wait half so long!"

She stared at him. "You asked *me* to wait these two years, William."

"Well, yes, but that was different, don't you see? Because we always had our understanding and have always been more like friends than . . . than anything else. When I met Rose, I knew right off we were just—that you and I had never been—Oh, everything is so different with Rose! She's the daughter of a merchant, a supplier at Gibraltar, and so—so perfectly beautiful! You'll see how wonderful she is when you meet her. If I'd left her, I knew I could not keep her. Two other fellows were hard on my heels, but she chose me." He straightened his shoulders. "We shall take a house at Portsmouth, and then she thinks I ought to stay with the Navy, or at least in shipping. So we shan't be up north to Brinford at all. Mama and Father shall visit us at Portsmouth. I knew you would understand, Marian, if I could just speak with you."

She still stared at him. "But this is not—not what you planned," she said. "All these years, you've spoken so fondly of Brinford, as though you hoped never to leave it!"

"I know!" William had started to pace. "I know that, Marian. But everything with Rose is—well, it simply happened. I did not plan it. And now all I seem to do is plan—to please her! She is the most perfect darling! I love her so—I only want what she wants."

And yet you would have had me retire to the country and abandon my painting, Marian thought, with a swift recognition that neither of them had ever loved each other as they ought. Though she knew herself better out of the arrangement, though she felt a lightening of her heart, knowing that William's announcement had spared her one of her own, she was still left to deal with a very public abandonment. And the repercussions for her were likely to be much more enduring than they ever would have been for William.

She permitted herself a spurt of resentment. She had thought better of William. But this was, after all, what she had wanted.

"I do not fault you, William, for your feeling. I know you did not seek it, nor yield without struggle. There is no reason, no . . . explanation behind much attraction. You love her, and there is naught that might now be changed about your marriage. But you must see that you've placed me in a most difficult position. Many here were aware of my engagement. 'Twas widely known."

William again turned red. "I know I should have come ahead and spoken to you first, that you should have been seen as releasing me first from any—any obligation. That you should have been let to cry off. But Rose pleaded so . . ."

"She knew of our engagement?"

"Oh, yes. But she also knew that we were rather more friends than—than closer; I had to tell her that, as you know it to be true, don't you, Marian? And she knows of your art, and she said you should be able to find work of some sort, then, or stay here with your cousins, who must be rather plump in the pockets, given this place. Or you might even return to Michael. So it is not really so bad, you see."

But most ungallant, Marian thought silently. And she decided she did not much care for the ambitious young Mrs. Reeves, much as she wished William well.

She attempted a smile. "There is little to be done now, William, except for me to wish you happy. I'd have preferred you had written me when you wrote Michael. But at least he directed you to me here in town. For I do need one favor from you." She sighed deeply. " 'Twould be much better for me if you concealed the marriage from our acquaintance for at least a few days. I know it cannot be hidden long—"

"I fear it cannot be hidden at all, Marian, for of course I had to send word to my parents on my arrival. Everyone in Brinford shall probably know today—or tomorrow at the latest."

"I see." She worried her lower lip. "But perhaps the news might be delayed here in town. If we do not tell my cousins just yet . . ." She scarcely knew why she troubled to delay, other than to postpone dealing with her future until she could quite accommodate the present. And somewhere in her confusion she wondered about Lord Sidley. She did not want him to know; William's defection deprived her of standing in society—Sidley's society. What must he make of her now—not only the Formsbys' poor relation but tossed over by her fiancé?

"Some officers from the *Perseus* are like to come on to town soon, Marian. There's to be an assembly of the fleet at Spithead, to impress the Prince Regent's foreign visitors. I fear I cannot keep this business quiet."

She nodded and rather numbly and pointlessly began toying with one of her brushes. Edith and Katie were due back at any moment.

"I think, William, that you had best leave now. You'll want to be getting back to your—to Rose as soon as possible. And I have much to consider—how to tell Edith, for one. It might be awkward, should you stay."

"I'll be off, then, Marian. I shall write you all about

everything. I must tell you all about my Rose! But first you must—I'd ask that you forgive me. You know I would never have hurt you. And I hope we might remain friends. You and Michael and I have always been family. I should like Rose to know you."

"Of course," she said, though she thought the relationship destined to be strained. "Do hurry now, William."

He moved with alacrity then to try to take her hand once more. But she hid it, protected, behind her back as she held the brush and let him graze her cheek with a swift kiss instead. In his actions he seemed more like a jubilant, ill-trained pet than the serious young sailor to whom she had been faithful for so long.

She did not walk him to the door. Instead she stood staring at her portrait of Lord Sidley. She silently asked his bright gaze for any guidance he might render. But those blue eyes looked strangely amused and superior. They lacked the understanding she knew they had often held for her. The flaw was one she had not caught until that moment, and she set about at once to earn Sidley's fancied sympathy by correcting his expression.

He could not bear the fellow. Lieutenant Reeves had to be got rid of. The question was how to do so respectably.

"You are looking very sour," Vaughn remarked. "Should I suspect the beer at the Guildhall last night?"

"I cannot recall any beer last night, or much else of the

meal, for that matter. 'Twas an outlandish crush. This season will be remarked years hence for its excesses. But Prinny will have it . . ."

"What has you looking so grim, then?"

"I have just met Lieutenant Reeves." Sidley glanced quickly at Vaughn, then looked away. "He does not deserve her."

"That was understood, of course. I thought you meant to surprise me."

"'Twould lighten my spirits to be rid of him."

"Shall I toss him into the Thames for you?"

"I would not have Miss Ware upset."

"I was not serious."

"I was." Sidley's gaze followed the couples dancing a reel. Yet for all the attention he paid them, they might have been in another country. If he had not promised to escort his aunt and Clara Poole to this party hosted by their friends, the Holnotts, Sidley would have much preferred to stay home and plan. But he had been obliged to attend. At least Clara was smiling again. He could be grateful for that.

"All these diversions—dining and drinking and skipping about . . ." Sidley muttered.

"It is called dancing. And you used to enjoy it well enough."

"Well enough? 'Tis many weeks since I've enjoyed anything about this infernal season."

"At least it shall be your last."

Sidley fixed Vaughn with a very determined eye. "You dare to be clever, my friend?"

"Not at all. I know your purpose. You shall be riveted to someone by fall whether you love or not. Either way, next season is unlikely to tempt you. By the by, is that old Colonel Bassett with your aunt? He does not appear to know the steps."

"She will tutor him," Sidley commented idly. His thoughts were once again on Lieutenant Reeves. One might, he supposed, appeal to the fellow's pocketbook—or to his ambition. Naval promotions were difficult to come by; aspiring junior officers were said to pray for war or plagues to open the ranks. But surely in these peaceful days, there must be many cutting loose? He could have Reeves made an admiral and sent half the world away.

"At least," Vaughn said, "we have rid ourselves of the responsibility of Benny."

Sidley nodded. His Grace the Duke of Derwin was delighted with his youngest son's purchase of a commission.

"Benny's unlikely to come to any harm at this point," Sidley said. "The House Guards shall stay safely in town, where he might parade about at any hour." He watched Lady Katherine enter the ballroom on Lord Carroll's arm.

"You should consider that another accomplishment," Vaughn said softly, indicating Katie with a lift of his chin.

"Perhaps. All tends to a close of sorts." As Sidley observed Lady Katherine, he wondered if Lieutenant Reeves had stayed the rest of the evening at the Formsbys'. He steeled himself to see the lieutenant enter the room next, with Marian Ware as his partner. But the couple did not attend. He told himself he was relieved—until he pictured them happily occupied at home. Excusing himself abruptly from Vaughn's company, he sought out Lady Katherine.

She appeared flustered at his approach. No doubt she viewed him now as an encumbrance, one that could only serve to interfere with her pursuit of Lord Carroll. Except, of course, that his competing attentions might prove invaluable in bringing Carroll to the point.

Sidley bowed to her brother, Formsby, then took Lady Katherine's hand for the lightest of feather kisses.

"Dearest Lady Katherine, you outshine the rest of this party."

"Lord Sidley," she acknowledged. "You remember Lord Carroll?"

"Indeed." He bowed to Carroll. Sidley hoped he conveyed the right parts of distance and humility. Carroll had to be treated as a respected rival, not the witless wastrel that he was. But Carroll, being witless, was not to apprehend his fate.

"Carroll, I fear I am not yet well enough to steal one of Lady Katherine's dances from you."

"Well, I—I . . ."

"But perhaps you would be kind enough to surrender

her to me for a mere ten minutes? I promise I will return her to you promptly."

"Well, I—"

"You do not mind, my lord?" Katie batted her lashes at Carroll, who looked delighted to have even so slight a decision sought.

"Your wish, my lady," he said, and smiled sweetly as he bowed.

Sidley hated to separate the two, but he needed information. He led Katherine along the perimeter of the dancers, toward the supper room.

"It is difficult to contend with such a dashing cove as Carroll," he confessed. "I hear all the young ladies consider him quite the catch."

"Oh, I have heard that as well! But then, you once— you are also quite admired, my lord."

"You are too kind, Lady Katherine. You must know I feel my age, particularly in company with young Carroll. He will be able to dance for many, many more years."

"I have seen older gentlemen dancing on occasion. Look at Colonel Bassett!"

Sidley preferred not. "Just so, Lady Katherine. Only on occasion, though," he sighed. "When their spirits are unusually high. And most of *them* needn't master a limp."

She frowned and looked away, as though she acknowledged the impediment as insurmountable.

"You are riding again, Lord Sidley," she said in encouragement. "Edgar told me he met you in the park just this morning."

"I have to take that small bit of exercise, Lady Katherine. I fear I must surrender driving a carriage forever, as my arms are still too weak to manage the ribbons. Perhaps Lord Carroll might take us up sometime, as I understand he is an excellent whip."

"To be sure, he is! Why, the other day we went so fast, I almost lost my newest bonnet! Everyone was plunging to the side!"

Sidley smiled sadly as they reached a table of refreshments. He handed a glass of punch to Katherine. "I find that speed often makes me quite queasy these days, Lady Katherine. If Lord Carroll does consent to ferry us, we must plead with him to drive slowly."

Katie frowned. "Perhaps we should not go out with Lord Carroll, then."

"But he seems most amiable."

"Oh, he is! But I could not ask him to—to—"

"Drive in such a sedate manner?"

Katie nodded.

"Then sometime he might accompany us on a walk. Or better yet, we might all sit together. I have never asked—are you fond of needlework, Lady Katherine?" As just then the dancers were engaged in another lively reel, Sidley could barely keep his countenance as he watched Katie's reaction. He suspected that she had at last struck him from her prospects.

"Well, no matter," he said cheerfully. "Perhaps you also do some drawing, as does your cousin? When we sit together, you might draw, while Lord Carroll and I discuss the drainage of fields."

"I have never had much patience for drawing, my lord," Katherine said, taking another gulp of punch and looking longingly at the joyous group of dancers. Lord Carroll, his magnificent blond mane shining in the lamplight, was notably one of them.

"Ah! Well, I imagine that Lieutenant Reeves must be most content to be home at last and watching Miss Ware draw. Although I did expect they might attend tonight. Or did Miss Ware have yet another lesson?"

"No, she was—" To his surprise, Lady Katherine again looked flustered. "She told us this afternoon that he had left."

"Left? To precede her to Northampton?"

"I don't know quite where he's gone, my lord. But . . . well . . ." She lowered her voice. "I suppose I might tell *you,* as you know her so well, and as it will all be out soon enough, about Marian's—about her disappointment. She was looking very pale. It must be so distressing! I know that *I* should have been much beside myself—after two years too! She did ask that we not speak of it for a few days. But as you have always been so kind to Marian, my lord, about her painting, and the portrait—"

"Spare the saints!" In his impatience he spoke too loud. As Katie glanced uncomfortably at the startled faces about them, he leaned closer. "What has happened?"

"She seemed most calm about it, my lord. Though it must have been such a shock. William has cried off! He married someone else, someone named Rose, two months ago in Gibraltar, without letting on to Marian at all. He wrote her brother, Michael. And Michael told him he should come along to see Marian the minute he docked, although of course he must have dreaded doing so. But 'twas the honorable thing to do, was it not?"

"Honorable!" Again he spoke too loudly. But he was amazed that he spoke at all. He was wild with glee. He wanted to kiss the thoughtless tattler before him. He wanted to leap into the midst of bounding dancers and plant Carroll a facer. He wanted to toss back his host's insipid punch as though it were the finest Champagne. Only effort kept him from yelling aloud. His gaze sought Vaughn, whose own gaze narrowed as he left Lady Adeline and Clara and began to walk his way.

"Lady Katherine," Sidley managed. The desire to smile nearly choked him. "This is shocking news. Shocking! Lieutenant Reeves has behaved in a most unacceptable manner. His conduct is disgraceful. Miss Ware is to be pitied." *Though a less pitiable creature than Marian Ware is hard to imagine.* "She will rally. But it is imperative, absolutely imperative, Lady Katherine, that you not say one word more to anyone—no one at all, not even Lord Carroll." He laid one finger lightly against her lips. "It is not in your cousin's best interest. And you must not tell *her* that you have informed *me*. She must not feel embarrassed or pitied in any way, because—because it is important that she be able to complete the portrait. That is my main concern. You understand?"

What utter balderdash!

"Yes," Katie said dubiously, "I see. Of course you wish it finished. And Marian is always happiest when she is painting."

Happiest—yes, he thought. *Out of the mouths of babes.* And at once he saw his way clear.

"Lady Katherine, you are a gem," he said, raising her gloved hand for a kiss. "Bless you." She glowed as he walked her back to Formsby. "You will remember what we discussed, Lady Katherine, will you not?" She nodded absently. Lord Carroll had not finished his dance. Katie's gaze already followed her favorite in his exertions. But Sidley believed he might rely upon her—for perhaps a day at most.

Vaughn met him as he moved to the hall and escape. "What's toward?" he asked. "You look the very devil, Sidley."

"She is free, Vaughn."

"Free? Miss Ware?"

Sidley nodded as he collected his hat and gloves. "If you would, kindly see Clara and Lady Adeline home. I've a small matter to attend to just now. Not a word, please."

Vaughn did not quite grin, though one eyebrow quirked expressively. But before Sidley could take his leave, a coachman came running up the steps to the door to confront the butler, the footmen, and Sidley.

"Here, you blokes—ah, sir—milord," he gasped. "I saw the lights. Thought as you might help. There's been a dreadful wreck. Up at the square. Lord Addlestrop's landau and my, that is—Mr. Knox's carriage. I fear Mr. Knox is very bad indeed. And there's a lady . . ."

"Mrs. Knox?" Sidley asked sharply as Vaughn surged to his side.

"Ah, no, milord. Not the missus. Some—some other—"

Sidley pushed Vaughn back into the hall. "You must stay here," he snapped. "You mustn't be involved."

And Vaughn nodded grimly as Sidley raced down to the street.

Chapter Eleven

Edgar called Marian to the study in the morning. Since she had advised her cousins only the previous evening of her broken betrothal, she expected Edgar to speak to her regarding her future. And as she had spent a sleepless night considering that very future, she now faced the meeting with a lingering megrim and considerable trepidation. She knew she would have no alternative if Edgar were to suggest, however kindly, that she return home to Brinford.

But to her relief, Edgar did not look worried or resigned. He held a letter, which he perused repeatedly and with obvious astonishment.

"Marian," he said, his eyebrows high as he waved the missive in front of her, "I had no idea! Five hundred guineas! 'Tis what Prinny shall give Lawrence for his portraits of the tsar and the king of Prussia!"

"I had no notion. But, Edgar, what five hundred guineas?"

"*Your* five hundred guineas, Marian! Sidley has deposited five hundred guineas at Drummond's Bank in your name. You need only sign for the sum. 'Tis payment for his portrait, and an advance for one of Mrs. Knox."

"Mrs. Knox?"

"He wants a portrait of Mrs. Knox as well. You mean you did not know?" As Marian shook her head, he added, "Perhaps you should not rely on that part of the payment, then. For there was a carriage accident last night, Marian, and Knox could not be saved."

"How awful! And Mrs. Knox?"

"The missus wasn't there, apparently, though Knox had company. And Mama's friend Lady Addlestrop was injured in the other carriage. I sent 'round for news earlier. . . . But as to this, Marian, whatever Sidley may have settled with Knox—well, we must sort that out. Seems to me, though, that even *half* of five hundred guineas is a considerable sum."

"It is too much—"

"You did not arrange it?"

"We spoke of a commission. I knew he would pay me—"

"If I invest this for you—or Michael does, of

course—you shall have a small income, on top of that bit from your portion. And if *others* should want a portrait—"

"Then I would like to make some restitution to you and Aunt Edith, Edgar."

"Oh, bosh, Marian! Mother and I discussed it last night. You are family. You must stay with us. 'Tis absurd to think you should pay for your tea and jam. You won't want to be back in Brinford just now anyway, with all of this upset over Reeves. And Mother would rather you kept company with Katie in any event."

"That is very good of you, Edgar. Though I shouldn't wish to impose. And if I keep these funds from Lord Sidley, given the cost of my lessons, I must certainly give you—"

"*If* you keep it? Why, of course you must keep it! Sidley's pleased with the work, else he wouldn't have convinced the 'Gruff'un' to part with so much of the ready. And I must say, Sidley has more to hand than any of us supposed. What's to frown about, Marian? Of course we'll have to look into this Knox portrait. Mrs. Knox won't want herself done up in mourning. But, otherwise, you should be fit to fly!"

"I am. I am. I—" She was just then comprehending the staggering size of the payment. "I needn't marry at all."

Edgar shot her a quizzical look. "But you will, of course. Everyone does. 'Tis expected. Though you're unlikely to do so now, certainly, for a bit. Reeves did you no favor there, Marian. Mother's quite cross with him. I'd no idea"—he waved the letter once more, ignoring Lieutenant Reeves's failings for the much happier development—"that portraits were so much the thing."

"'Tis an excessive amount, Edgar. You mustn't think anyone else would be so generous."

"All the same, once this gets about—"

"I shouldn't wish it to just yet. Do you understand? With William, and then Mr. Knox's passing, I shall be rather infamous."

"All the better!"

"Oh, Edgar!"

He looked a bit shamefaced. And just as Marian wished Edith were present, Edith arrived—to exclaim over Lord Sidley's gesture and then to claim that it must indicate a desire to align himself with the family.

"That can't be so, Mama," Edgar protested. "He's been seen more frequently of late in Miss Poole's company than Katie's, and if Katie's serious about Sidley, she's goin' about it in a very odd manner. Steppin' out with Carroll—"

"Your sister has not been 'stepping out' with Lord Carroll," Edith reproved him.

"Now, you must admit that Katie's smitten with Carroll, Mama. Making a cake of herself, if you ask me. And the bettin' books at the clubs—"

"I will not have it, Edgar! Such wagers are not to be taken seriously."

Edgar withdrew somewhat mulishly. And as he stood idly fingering Sidley's letter, Marian asked if she might see it.

The note was brief and most unsatisfactorily terse:

Formsby
My lord,

As Miss Ware has substantially completed the portrait I commissioned from her, I have arranged for the sum of five hundred guineas to be available upon her signature and presentation of this letter at Drummond's; this amount in final payment for the finished portrait and one additional, to be executed within the next twelvemonth, of Mrs. Griffin Knox.

Yours & c.
Sidley

He had stamped it with a crest, which Marian examined with some curiosity. She had never before read his hand.

"Marian," Edith said, drawing her bemused attention, "are you quite all right?"

"Yes, Aunt."

"And Edgar told you of Mr. Knox's accident last night?"

"Only that there was such an accident, and that as Mrs. Knox is now a widow, the commission may not still be desired."

"I've just sent 'round to Addlestrop's, Mama," Edgar

said, "to inquire after Lady Addlestrop. She is not do-ing well. They've called for a physician."

"Goodness! Poor Beulah. That such a thing should happen to her, who has such fragile nerves!"

"Not so surprising, Mama, when Addlestrop insists on putting that demented nag in the traces. The—horse, I mean, Mama. Their coachman said Knox would not yield, and he couldn't."

"Oh, dear. I must attend Beulah. Marian, I know you go to your lessons, but I must have the carriage. Edgar shall walk over with you and the maid. Never fear, I shall send the carriage 'round for you later. Oh, why is Katie never up 'til three?"

And as Edith rushed to ready herself, Marian left with Edgar, to spend their walk correcting his impres-sion that she now need never take another class. She told her tutors, without explanation, that she hoped to remain in town a few weeks longer and then attempted to draw, with a remarked lack of success. Though she knew her situation happier than it had been the day be-fore, though she usually forgot herself in her work, so much remained unsettled that she could not feel quite content. She had planned that from this summer on, her future would be William's, but now that she was to stay with her cousins, her plans must align with theirs. Just how long such an arrangement might prove agreeable seemed most uncertain. And she was wishing fervently that her future might at last be entirely her own.

She was still mulling over her good fortune and its

unexpected complications when she returned later that afternoon. Since she heard company in the west drawing room, she left her supplies for the maid to take on upstairs and removed her bonnet as she crossed the hall to greet Edith's guests.

Inside the room her cousins were entertaining a score of callers, among them Lord Sidley, Lord Vaughn, and Clara Poole.

"I believe you know everyone, Marian," Edith said, and Marian curtsied in acknowledgment. But her gaze was solely for Sidley and Lord Vaughn. For though Vaughn was used to appearing entirely solemn, he was now grinning broadly, and Sidley, whose health had so visibly improved over the past two weeks, appeared again to be ailing.

Marian frowned and moved toward him, only to be intercepted by Clara.

"Miss Ware," she said, "I'm so pleased to see you today. I had hoped to meet with you again at the Holnotts' party last night."

Marian explained, without truly explaining, why she had not attended the party with her cousins. Though she had been immensely relieved by William's visit, it had been followed by an unrelieved headache, which fact she could relay in all truth. Marian liked Clara Poole, but at the moment she wished only to reach the opposite side of the room and Sidley. Thankfully, Edith chose to address Clara just then on some point relating to Dicky Poole's engagement, and Marian excused herself.

She dearly wished to speak to him—to acknowledge his payment, to protest it, to thank him—but though Sidley had often approached her in the past, he did not do so now. He was frustratingly aloof. And she noticed with some dismay that his portrait had been brought down from her room upstairs and placed in one corner on display.

She did not think he would care for that—indeed, he did not look as though he cared for it at all.

"Marian is so clever," Katie was saying for the whole company. "Isn't it wonderful?"

Oh, please, Katie, Marian thought, *not now.* There was much chatter, much commendation, as Marian made her way to Sidley. She noticed with proximity just how pale and tired he looked.

"Are you well, my lord?"

"We have established that I am." His eyes did not reflect his smile. At her impatient glance he added, "Forgive me. I did not sleep last night. You will have heard there was an accident outside the Holnotts' party, and Griffin Knox was killed. Given the number of revelers these days, the streets are unsafe at all hours. One can only do what one must. . . ." His voice trailed off. He was looking not at her but at Katie as she gushed to her callers.

Marian suspected that Lord Sidley had been called upon more frequently than anyone realized—and that he did more than most surmised.

"It sounds horrific," she said.

"Yes."

"My lord, I must suppose then that I—that is, I must presume that I will no longer be painting Mrs. Knox."

Sidley turned to look more fully at her. "Knox did not request a portrait. I did."

"*You* did?"

Once again his gaze surveyed the Formsbys' guests. "Some years ago," he said, "Griffin Knox bought Jenny Lanning—or as near as one might still come in these isles to purchasing another. How a man could then be so jealously possessive of what he'd bought, yet mistreat her so, was a mystery to me. And very hard on my friend Vaughn there." Sidley raised his chin toward Lord Vaughn. "I should like the portrait for him, as a gift. Jenny Knox is a lovely woman, and Vaughn is now in a position to gratify his heart. A most enviable situation. When the fates intervene, as they did last night, we must take advantage. Do you not think so?"

Though he was clearly tired, his gaze was at once very direct and searching. In the pause, Marian thought him expectant. And she was thinking that the fates *had* intervened—to free her from any obligation to William. But she could not tell Lord Sidley. She could not tell him, for fear of his pity. Her chin rose.

"My lord," she said urgently and very softly. "About your payment—I would speak with you."

"Are we not speaking now?" Again she noticed impatiently that the others in the room drew his attention. But when his gaze again sought her face, his look was steady. "I would rather not have the discussion you desire."

"But it is too much," she protested.

He smiled. "Should I not determine my own worth?" He gestured rather dismissively toward the portrait. "I expected you to reject the payment, but you mustn't. Surely you must welcome the provision, and the lieutenant must consider it opportune, with your nuptials so very near."

Again she thought his manner expectant.

"There has been . . . a delay," she admitted, swallowing.

"A delay? How unfortunate for him." He paused, the smile faded, and then he added carelessly, "The funds are yours. You must dispense with them as you see fit."

"But it really is too much. I haven't the reputation—"

"You might trust me to assure it." Though amusement laced his voice, he did not smile. "Where is Lieutenant Reeves this evening?" he asked.

"He has had to return to Portsmouth."

"So soon?" He held her gaze until Marian almost confessed. *He married another. He did not want me. But I do not want him. I want—*

Again the conversation and activity in the rest of the room distracted him, or perhaps he did not care to be observed in a *tête-à-tête* with her. They were not private, and they were interrupted.

"You must be very pleased with the portrait then,

Sidley?" Edgar asked, joining them with Clara Poole and Lord Vaughn.

"Most emphatically. Who had the thing brought down?"

"M'sister. She thought it might entertain."

"Indeed. There are few entertainments as diverting as admiring oneself."

"Lee!" Clara protested, in a manner that Marian thought most warm and familiar. Clara drew a smile from Sidley.

"Miss Ware is to be commended," he admitted more politely. "Though I might accuse her of flattering me. Clearly she draws too much upon the imagination."

"I have not yet finished, my lord," she said.

"Indeed? How long am I to be worked upon?" Though he asked lightly, Marian thought his gaze a challenge.

"Until she has improved you, Lee!" Clara admonished.

" 'Twill be an age, then," Sidley commented. "For by definition, 'tis well nigh impossible to improve upon the best." As Lord Vaughn huffed dismissively, Marian again held Sidley's gaze, wondering just what he might mean. That he himself could not be bettered, or her rendering of him?

"But I think I must shortly have the piece removed to Sidley House," he added. "If you are willing to part with it, Miss Ware? The original is, of course, always at your disposal."

As he gave her a shallow bow, Edgar remarked, "You've certainly paid for it an' all."

"Thank you," Sidley said dryly. "Though Miss Ware may claim the painting unfinished, it has eyes, nose, and mouth enough that I confess to feeling somewhat exposed."

As Lord Vaughn huffed once more, Clara said, "She has caught that look."

Sidley turned to her. "This is not the first time I have been accused of having a 'look,'" he said. "I note that no one dares define it in my presence."

"But Miss Ware has portrayed it most faithfully, my lord," Clara teased. "You have only to *look*!"

"Perhaps Miss Ware will describe her work to me."

"I only paint what I see, Lord Sidley, as I am not gifted with words."

"I should not have concurred before this afternoon," he said rather sharply. "Indeed, you have always proved most capable of expressing yourself. I recall one incident in particular, at Aldersham, that spoke volumes for your loquacity."

As her jaw dropped, he again surveyed the room and its cheerful occupants. He turned abruptly to Vaughn. "I believe we must be off, Vaughn. Clara?" He offered an arm to Clara. As he readied to depart, Marian, who was wishing she had more time or more courage, could only observe him. "Whatever the 'look,' Miss Ware, I acknowledge that you have captured it. You mustn't mind my ill humor. I am delighted with the portrait. I ask only that you do whatever else you feel you must do to it at Sidley House."

His manner was dismissive. She could not think of a thing to say.

"I fear we must be going. Formsby," he said loftily, acknowledging Edgar. And he and his party made their adieus to Katie and Edith.

Marian watched him leave, watched his height and elegantly clad breadth of shoulder depart, with some feeling of despair.

"Did you tell him?" Katie asked, immediately coming to Marian's side. "Is that why he looked so blue-deviled?"

"Tell him what, Katie?" she asked wearily. She had not said anything she wished to say. And she thought it likely that Clara Poole now had expectations. Yet Sidley had been so very strange . . .

"Why, that I should not wish to disappoint him. But that I, that is, with Carroll—"

"Katie, I did not speak of you."

Katie pouted. "What on earth were you discussing, then? All of us could see you, even from across the room—"

"The portrait! Always the portrait! What else would we discuss?"

Katie looked taken aback by her temper.

Marian quickly apologized and fled the room. The news would be out shortly. He would hear in any event. She questioned what she thought to preserve, other than a momentary pride. But to boldly state, *"I have been thrown over. I have been jilted,"* in front of a roomful of the *ton's* well-placed callers, did not appeal.

Only three hours later, even before dinner, two servants arrived from Sidley House with a horse-drawn wagon and instructions to collect "Miss Ware's painting." Though startled by the sudden removal, Marian believed she understood Sidley's preference. She was not assured, however, that the men would take the care they should with the wet oil paint; she did not trust the work, now so near completion, to travel safely. As her aunt and Katie were still dressing for dinner, Marian readied the piece, then summoned a maid and gathered her cloak.

"Marian, what are you about?" Edgar asked, entering the hall just as the painting was being carried out the door.

"I must see this over to Sidley House at Grosvernor Square. I shan't be gone long. But you mustn't wait dinner."

"But see here, I can't let you run off alone in the evening!"

"I've a maid with me, Edgar, and Lady Adeline and Miss Poole are at Sidley House. No one will remark it."

"All the same . . ."

"Edgar, please. If I go just now, I shall be back before you are all at table."

Frowning, with some mumbling about the "portrait trade," Edgar let her go. And Marian swiftly fled to the street, to climb atop the wagon seat and direct the placement of the painting. With the aid of one of the men, she then held it upright for the brief trip to Sidley's residence.

The town home astonished her, as it was large, beautifully detailed, and not, as Colonel Bassett had implied so many weeks before, "falling to ruin." As the wagon stopped before the gracefully curved front steps, Marian recalled her mission and stopped staring. Hopping down to the street, she directed the men to hand her the painting. And despite their protests, she said she would see it inside herself. Though she directed the servants around back, one of them insisted on helping her carry the half-length canvas up the steps before leaving Marian alone at the door.

"I am here for—I am here to see Lady Adeline," she improvised, at once awed by the soaring ceilings and stately sculptures in the hall and by the politely inquiring manner of the butler. She guessed she should not have come. But the butler showed her in more hospitably, Marian thought, than an uninvited visitor deserved at the dinner hour. Just seconds later, relieved of her cloak, she was escorted to a drawing room, where her gaze focused disbelievingly on the exquisite Holbein portrait over the mantel.

"Sidley's father purchased it more than thirty years ago, before his wedding," Lady Adeline told her, following her rapt gaze. The lady was dressed most elegantly. Perhaps they meant to go out. "There are not that many of them," she added.

"No," Marian breathed. "No." She swallowed. "Forgive me, ma'am, for the intrusion. But Lord Sidley sent for his portrait, and I found I did not trust entirely that it would travel safely. Shall I just leave it here?" She moved to stand the painting in its traveling frame against a side table. Above that same side table hung another dreamlike Claude landscape. In the presence of so much beauty Marian felt nearly numbed.

"You are most attentive, my dear," Lady Adeline said. "Though I assure you, the men are accustomed to transporting paintings."

"Yes. I can see that must indeed be the case." Marian eyed the drawing room's blue velvet drapes, dark walls, and extensive white and gilt moldings. In the fading evening sun the gold details reflected the light, making luminous the treasured oil paintings—as though they were aglow.

"This house is *beautiful*," she breathed, "Not 'falling to ruins' at all."

" 'Falling to ruins'! I should say not. Though Sidley has had to set some crews of plasterers and painters to work. Why on earth would you think otherwise?"

"I meant no affront, my lady. Colonel Bassett said—"

"Colonel Bassett, that old meddler! A most disappointed man, Miss Ware, who lost one very fine son and is left with the other, who is, perhaps, not as fine. But all of us have had disappointments. 'Tis no reason to cast aspersions."

"No, ma'am."

"Am I not permitted to see it then, Miss Ware?" Lady Adeline asked, gesturing toward Marian's portrait. "I understand you have been working since I last saw it."

"Certainly." Marian quickly leaned to unwrap the painting and free it from the embracing frame.

"Yes." Lady Adeline eyed it intently. "It is wonderful. You are pleased?"

"I am, my lady. Though there are still details I should like to finish." She smiled. "But surely the question is whether Lord Sidley is pleased?"

Lady Adeline returned the smile. "He would not have sent for it were he not pleased. Though his urgency does mystify . . ."

"I believe he chose not to have it, as a proxy for himself, attract such public scrutiny."

Lady Adeline lips twitched. "Did he not? How unusual." Again she studied the portrait. "It is excellent, Miss Ware. Beautifully composed and most professionally rendered. I must confess, though, to a slight preference for the other."

"The other?"

"The watercolor sketch."

"That was very quick. . . ."

"Whatever the method, it is perfect. Sidley is having it framed."

"Oh." Marian stood for a second at a loss for words. She had been fond of the watercolor. She had thought at first to keep it as a remembrance of Sidley. But she'd determined that retaining his company, in any form, was inadvisable.

"Your lessons do not continue much longer, I suppose,

Miss Ware?" his aunt asked. "Surely you are now qualified to give them?"

Marian smiled and shook her head. "It will take me many years to feel I master even a fraction of so much. But I shall probably continue with my tutors for another month at least. Until I depart with my cousins for Bath and their house at Enderby."

"You go to Bath with them? But surely Edith said—I believe your young lieutenant is expected to return shortly?"

"He has already returned, ma'am. Returned and departed." As Lady Adeline frowned, Marian breathed almost in relief. She was not comfortable with dissembling. "Lieutenant Reeves has married another, my lady. He was just in town yesterday to tell me. I am no longer betrothed."

"No longer—but, my dear, this is appalling!"

" 'Tis rather unsettling for me, certainly."

"But I mean, it is not done! 'Tis unconscionable behavior, and most hurtful."

Marian smiled. "I fear Lieutenant Reeves is beyond caring."

"You are too understanding, Miss Ware. You are not angry?"

"I am resentful, ma'am. I would have wished to end the engagement myself."

"Indeed?" Lady Adeline's glance was sharp. " 'Twas not a love match?"

"William was a friend of long-standing, my lady. My affections have been his for so many years that I cannot recall when I did not believe them fixed. I had thought such sufficient for marriage."

"It can be. It can be, my dear. But for one of your nature . . ." Her voice softened. "I have loved only one man in my life, Miss Ware. 'Tis no secret. I lost him at Guildford Courthouse—in the Carolina colonies—more than thirty years ago. There has never been another."

"I am sorry to hear that, my lady. He must have been extraordinary."

"Extraordinary? Yes, I thought him so. And together, I believe—perhaps we were extraordinary together." She rallied, clearing her throat. "So, you are no longer betrothed. What of your situation? What shall you do with yourself? Take more commissions for portraits?"

"I shall try to attract them, though I keep a home with my cousins." As Lady Adeline frowned once more, Marian said quickly, "I have intruded long enough here this evening, my lady. I see that you are going out. I shall take my leave." She bobbed and turned to go, but Lady Adeline came closer.

"Stay. Do stay, Miss Ware." If it were possible for so formidable a lady to look uncertain, Lady Adeline did. "We do not go out until after dinner. Will you not stay and join us? We have time to send a note 'round to Edith."

"I thank you, but I should not. I really only came because I was concerned—" As she glanced again at the portrait, Lady Adeline followed her gaze. For some seconds the two of them contemplated Sidley.

"Do you know what it is you have painted?" Lady Adeline asked at last. "I wonder if you do. Despite all the sadness in this family, *he* is determined to see it—the joy in life. He will not surrender it. 'Tis why others are attracted to him. Like moths to flame! He is not all shallow amusements and clowning about, Miss Ware. Though he *was* out all last night again. And here I thought he had settled." She spoke so reprovingly that Marian was moved to defend Sidley.

"There was an accident last night, ma'am. Fatal to one gentleman. I believe Lord Sidley lent a hand."

"Well, yes, he would, would he not? Though he never says a word to *me,* mind you. *I* am never out without an explanation."

"No, ma'am." Despite all, Marian could not hide her smile.

Lady Adeline observed her closely. "Tell me, Miss Ware, has your cousin Lady Katherine chosen Carroll?"

"I believe Lord Carroll interests her at the moment, ma'am. Though there is no understanding . . ."

"You needn't be so careful, my dear. I assure you, my nephew's heart is not engaged. Though I had hopes. I now believe his interest fixed in another quarter."

"Oh." Marian backed up two steps. "Please excuse me now, my lady—"

"Clara will be disappointed."

"Do convey my apologies."

"I think I shall enjoy having her at Aldersham, particularly if events unfold as I anticipate."

Marian's misery left her mute. She feared that the others might be down at any moment and again quickly bobbed a curtsey.

"Miss Ware, does Sidley know of Lieutenant Reeves's departure?"

Marian shook her head.

"You have not forgiven him?"

"Forgiven Lord Sidley, my lady?"

"For the misapprehension, for that silly hum about his state of health. He was never so done in. Edith told me all of you knew."

"Yes, my lady." Marian's chin rose. "Though 'tis very difficult to excuse such a hoax. His purpose still eludes me. I suppose no lasting harm has been done. Yet to devise such a deception, for any reason, much less his own entertainment—"

"Oh, but it was not Sidley's devising, my dear. He attempts to protect *my* reputation by withholding the truth. 'Twas my own doing. Not purposely, of course," she added at Marian's incredulous expression. "I sincerely thought him dead to me, or certainly nearly so. I was not entirely myself, Miss Ware, when I first saw him so ill. So very pale—laid out like a corpse! I have seen too many. And once the mistaken belief had circulated, we found it 'nigh impossible to counter. You must never permit yourself to become an object of speculation, Miss Ware. 'Tis a most unfortunate position."

"Such things cannot be helped, ma'am," Marian sighed. "My own position, with Lieutenant Reeves . . ."

Lady Adeline considered her. "If you should marry another, 'twill hardly be noted."

"I have been painting, my lady." Marian tried to smile. "I have not been accumulating prospects."

"No, no, of course not." Lady Adeline appeared to muse. "But weddings are such happy events. I am delighted to think that Clara shall at last be part of the family."

"Indeed?" Marian felt faint. "I like her very much. When is the—have they picked a day?"

"About six weeks from today, in early August, I believe. It is not enough time, but Richard is, of course, most enthusiastic, and her father has not objected."

"Her father already knows?" Marian had believed the Pooles' parents to be in India.

"Certainly. He was there when they announced." Observing Marian's face, she said, "There seems to be some confusion, Miss Ware. Of whom do you think I speak?"

"Why, of Clara and Lord Sidley, ma'am."

Lady Adeline looked most imperious. "Delia Tinckney-Dwight is a distant cousin of mine, Miss Ware, through her mother. When Delia marries Richard Poole, Clara will at last become a member of the family—in the broadest sense, of course. She and Simon had had an understanding, and Sidley and the Pooles have always been much like siblings."

"I see." Relief made her heart race. She bobbed dutifully and turned to go.

"Will you not stay to speak with him, Miss Ware?" Lady Adeline's voice had softened.

"Another time, perhaps, my lady. You are very kind, but I must not intrude. Lord Sidley would be put out."

"Put out! Miss Ware, I beg your pardon, but is that the impression he gives you? That he would be *inconvenienced*? Do you care nothing for him at all?"

At that Marian blushed. She could picture herself, in vivid shades of crimson, scarlet, rose. And as her discomfort soared, so did Lady Adeline's astonishment.

"My dear, forgive me—" she began, but they heard footsteps in the hall. As pink as Marian felt, she grew more so when Sidley's voice reached them.

"Auntie, when should you like—" And on entering the doorway, he halted abruptly.

Chapter Twelve

Sidley watched his aunt brush past him into the hall. Then he fixed an inquiring gaze on Marian. "Will she be returning?"

Marian shook her head, not in answer but in the absence of one. Sidley was not yet fully dressed. Though he wore a shirt and waistcoat, he was fastening cuffs at his wrist. And at his collar . . . He had no collar. He had not tied the cravat over his open throat.

He held her shocked gaze. "Bandling," he called over his shoulder, and the wiry little valet appeared from nowhere. "I need a coat."

"Yes, m'lord. The blue for painting, m'lord?"

"Miss Ware is not here to paint just now, Bandling. Any coat will do. I would spare the lady's blushes."

Swiftly the servant wheeled and departed.

"Do forgive me. I was not informed of company." As Sidley bowed to her, Marian managed to focus on his head of glossy black hair. She took a deep breath. She still felt the warmth in her cheeks. "I came with the painting," she said in a rush.

"Ah, yes! I should have expected you to fuss with the thing."

"The 'thing,' my lord? You do not sound as though you care much for the 'thing' at all."

"I care more for the painter than the painting, that is certainly true."

She stared at him. Confronting him here in the hall, though such an event should not have been unexpected, seemed to addle her wits.

"Miss Marian." He was most courteously indicating the drawing room behind her. "Won't you please have a seat?"

"You are about to have dinner."

"Not at all." He smiled, as though aware that he disputed the obvious. "The meal can wait. And in any event, this no longer can."

Believing she heard an ominous stress on the word *this,* Marian turned with some resolve to take a seat at the fireside beneath the magnificent Holbein. When she glanced at Sidley, who had followed her to the hearth, she noticed he had managed, quickly and adeptly, to toss his linen into something resembling a cravat. The valet raced in behind him. As Marian focused on some point beyond Sidley's left shoulder, he shrugged into his coat, leaving it unbuttoned. She had never before seen him dressed in less than sartorial splendor, but his present informality scarce detracted.

"That will be all, Bandling," Sidley told the valet, though he did not look to him. Sidley's gaze was entirely on Marian. "And, Bandling, shut the door."

At once Marian protested. "My lord—"

"You mustn't cavil, my dear, as you were so bold as to come here unaccompanied. And you are in no danger. There are two other respectable ladies in this household who may enter the room at will."

"You take liberties," she said, even as he settled into the seat opposite.

"Surely not. This is my home."

"Then I must leave." She rose to her feet.

Sidley winced as he also rose. "I wish you would not, Miss Marian, as we have much to discuss and never seem to be left to do so."

"Anything you say might be said as easily with the door open."

"But I am much more likely to be understood with the door closed." At her frown he indicated the chair once again. "Please."

Marian returned to her seat. As she did so, her glance strayed nervously to the Holbein.

"You like that portrait?" Sidley asked.

"How could I not? You must know it is superb. Unique and superb."

Sidley observed her closely. "You share something

of his skill. Oh, not in style, of course," he said, dismissing her immediate objection, "but in a certain frankness. An honesty of portrayal. I might even term it *sincerity*, Marian. A sincerity that, unfortunately, does not appear to convey to your private affairs." As Marian once again moved as though to stand, Sidley held up a palm. "But you are here now," he conceded, "which is a promising start."

Marian's chin rose. "Lord Sidley, I have often been in your debt—"

"A position you have sorely resented."

"No, I—"

"Come, my dear. Do you believe me a stranger to my own devices? You are a most levelheaded young woman. Indeed, were you less so, I suspect I'd not be half as enchanted."

She could not have heard him aright. "My lor—"

"I do wonder at your reticence now, though, Marian. I think I must have come to rely upon your candor, however unsettling to my peace. I've had great hopes for your eagerness to share some news with me. Perhaps you attempt to spare my feelings? Or do you believe I have none worth informing?"

"I will not stay so that you might sharpen your wits—"

"I'm gratified that you grant me any, given the way in which you confound them."

"Surely for *you* to require frankness from *me* is outside of enough! You have no call to be angry."

"Angry? My dear Marian, this afternoon, at your

cousins', I was disappointed, wholly frustrated, and at the moment I am certainly impatient. But not angry. I am rarely angry. And when I am, I do not sit and discuss it. Is your Lieutenant Reeves often angry?"

"William? Why, he—" She caught his look and stopped abruptly. "You know."

"Yes."

"Katie?"

Sidley smiled. "Lady Katherine is most forthcoming. Unlike her cousin."

"I would have told you."

"When?"

"As soon as I had arranged my future." She thought his eyes looked very blue. She had not painted them blue enough.

"Do you know, I have been regretting my artifice," he said easily, though the intensity in his gaze remained. "Regretting it only with respect to you, my dear—until today, when it became clear that your own surpassed mine."

"*My* artifice?"

"Certainly. Which exceeds mine, because yours is rehearsed. You would have me believe you do not care for me at all, when you know that is simply not the case."

"Not care for—Why, what abominable pride!" Again she popped to her feet. "Must Lord Sidley command everyone's affections, as well as all their attention?"

He obligingly stood as well. "Not everyone's, Marian. Just yours." As she gazed at him, he moved closer, to the fireside between them, and placed one hand upon the mantel. "That is, of course, only possible if your affections are not still engaged elsewhere? I find I must fight the impulse to call the lieutenant out—he has not behaved at all well. And if he has hurt you, his actions are doubly reprehensible. Still, though you find yourself temporarily at a loss, I cannot help but recognize the man has done *me* a monumental favor."

"It would not be your place, my lord, to call Lieutenant Reeves out. . . ."

"Not yet, certainly," he inserted, leading her to glance at him warily.

"And as for hurting me, I *was* astonished. I should have wondered at myself had I not been. His marriage was most unexpected. But my feelings were . . . that is, I think that perhaps he must have performed a favor for me as well."

"How so, my dear?"

"Why, if he did not care for me enough to be true, then I am better unwed. And he has left me free to pursue my painting. With the payment you have made me, if I am careful, I needn't consider marriage at all."

He sighed. "There was that risk, of course."

"What risk, my lord?"

"Had you been alone, and poor, you might have been receptive to another offer."

"Lady Adeline mentioned the same. I have not been in the marriage mart. And I am not so calculating."

"Not calculating, Marian. Merely practical."

"Why must you call me Marian? You should not. . . ."

"You must call me Sidley. Or better yet, Lee. Or perhaps something of your own devising, since I am to be your patron."

"My patron! My lord, I have finished with you."

His gaze narrowed. "And now you are much too blunt, my dear. Need I remind you that you are contracted to paint Jenny Knox?"

"I meant—I misspoke, my lord. I meant that I am not your obligation."

"Indeed? Yet I feel I have an obligation, one of sensibility if nothing else. I owe much to our understanding, which I believe is considerable. You have not lived long enough, my dearest Marian, to realize that such understanding is too rare to be dismissed."

"But I do not need a patron."

She thought he smiled, though his lips did not move.

"Given your confidence, perhaps you never will. But is some aid not preferable to employment as a copyist, or retiring to quaint little Brinford to paint ladies' fans?" As her lips set stubbornly, he smiled openly. "Come, sweet, what is your objection? That *your* pride confuses patronage with pity? That as a woman and—pardon me—a spinster, any help from a gentleman must appear unseemly? Or do you object because I am in love with you?" As she stared at him, he repeated, "I am in love with you, yes. I have been courting you, in my fashion, since I first saw you."

"In . . . your *fashion*! Whilst you have been openly

wooing several others! Others much more eligible than myself to serve as respectable consort to Lord Sidley!"

He shrugged but retained his smile. "I should never have described them so. You did have a most inconvenient fiancé. And I did not woo them, Marian. I reviewed them. I chose to please my aunt."

"Lady Adeline! What must *she* think of such an arrangement?"

"Do sit, Marian. Please." As she backed to the chair and collapsed into it, he asked, "Can you truly be so surprised? Have I not made my preference all too clear? I thought myself as obvious as the weather."

"I thought I—I thought I must have imagined much."

He smiled. "I confess I also imagined much. Shall I tell you what I imagined as you painted—all those hours at Aldersham? I had to focus my thoughts as well as my gaze upon the poetry books behind you, else I should have gone mad with wanting to leap up and kiss you."

As she straightened, he placed one finger lightly against his lips. "Pray bear with me, dearest, and permit me to do this properly. Tradition requires your patience for just one minute more. So"—he cleared his throat—"Greene's lines must serve me. '*Oh, glorious sun*'—meaning *you,* of course, with your pride and talent and, yes, apparent tendency to temper—'*imagine me the west*'" He tapped his chest. "'*Shine in my arms*'" He generously opened both palms to her. "'*And set thou in my breast.*' Rather a wish than a command, you see, and—as to the location of the heart—self-explanatory."

That was enough. At the look on her face he instantly took the two steps to her chair and carefully knelt on one knee before her. He could not have done so as easily, she realized, had his coat been properly buttoned.

"Dearest Marian, I need only have you come home to me." He reached to cradle her limp hands. "You've lovely, capable hands. . . ." He raised them to the warmth of his lips, then pressed her unresisting fingers to his chest. ". . . and a prodigious talent. But so have I—for appreciating it. I shall never impede you. I've a persistent belief we shall get on well together. Will you do me the great honor, the inestimable honor, of becoming my wife?"

"To *marry* you? You intend that I should be—"

"Lady Sidley. Yes. Shall you mind very much?"

"But you cannot want this! Your family—"

"As I am the last of it, I am free to set its course. My aunt dotes upon you in any event. And, Marian . . ." His gaze was very bright. Indeed, he was so close that she could read her own reflection in his eyes. "Why should I not want your passion and purpose? They speak well of your capacity. In time, you might even come to love me."

"But I love you now! I quite adore you, as I suspect you well know. I have been sick at heart, because you must look higher. You are an earl! I am not right for you. We cannot do this." A gentle tug drew her protesting lips to his. "There will be talk," she whispered weakly.

"My love," he said, moving to kiss her. "We do not care. We shall not be here to listen."

True to his word, Lord Sidley missed the greater part of the following year in London, having taken his bride on an extended tour of the Continent's neglected treasures. The two returned in the spring, to a triumphant viewing of Lady Sidley's paintings in the next Royal Academy exhibition. But the much-discussed likeness of the earl was not among them. For, despite rumors that the portrait hung privately at Sidley House, the countess continued to claim that her meager talent could never do her husband justice.